'Uniquely Australian and uncommonly good, I could hear the author's voice in every spare, haunting line. More please.'

— Michael Robotham

'My friend Bryan Brown, quite apart from his other manifold talents, turns out to be an excellent writer. An authentic voice; highly imaginative yet completely believable, with a flair for fully realised characters and a gripping narrative . . . a great story teller. This is utterly baffling. I'm furious.'

— Sam Neill

'Bryan Brown makes an impressive entry into Australian literary ranks with his first collection of short stories . . . A terrific collection of gritty tales, recommended.'

—*Canberra Weekly*

'Brutally funny and distinctively Australian . . . Bryan Brown is going to be a force to be reckoned with on the literary scene.'

—*Woman's Day*

'Dazzling . . . strikingly original. If Brown ever decides to leave acting there is clearly another career waiting for him.'

—*The Sydney Morning Herald*

'A colourful, bold and cheeky ~~. . .~~ f suburban Aussie noir storie

—Book'd Out

BRYAN BROWN is known as an actor, having appeared in over eighty film and television shows. He has worked in some twenty countries including his home country of Australia and the United States.

Sweet Jimmy, consisting of seven short stories on crime, was released in 2021. An extract from his new book, *The Drowning*, is included at the back of this book.

SWEET JIMMY

Thanks to the family

BRYAN BROWN

CRIME HAS MANY FACES...
REVENGE IS ONE

SWEET JIMMY

ALLEN & UNWIN
SYDNEY · MELBOURNE · AUCKLAND · LONDON

Allen & Unwin
Cammeraygal Country
83 Alexander Street
Crows Nest NSW 2065
Australia
Phone: (61 2) 8425 0100
Email: info@allenandunwin.com
Web: www.allenandunwin.com

Allen & Unwin acknowledges the Traditional Owners of the Country on which we live and work. We pay our respects to all Aboriginal and Torres Strait Islander Elders, past and present.

A catalogue record for this book is available from the National Library of Australia

ISBN 978 1 76147 033 2

Set in Sabon LT Pro by Midland Typesetters, Australia
Printed and bound in Australia by Pegasus Media & Logistics

10 9 8 7 6 5 4

CONTENTS

BOYS WILL BE KILLERS

It was a gentle knock.

Agnes had been waiting for it. Hoping he would be on time.

Such a lovely fella she thought.

That's why the kettle was on, with a freshly baked sponge cake on the table.

'Feed the man meat' was a silly expression. Where did it come from? Who knew? Should be 'Feed the man cake'.

He'd have time for that before he began.

Agnes beamed as she opened the door to him: 'So punctual.'

He smiled.

'Come on through. Got a surprise for you,' she said.

He had one for her too.

——

There were three of them. Two were brothers, Johnny and Jimmy. The third was an older cousin, Phil. By five years.

They were Eastern Suburbs boys. Coogee.

It was the mid-seventies and, even though The Beatles had elbowed The Beach Boys off the charts, the beach was still the place to be.

But not for Johnny, Jimmy and Phil. They didn't surf. They thieved.

Phil' started when he was fifteen. He'd wander into Surf, Dive and Ski or David Jones, try on a jacket and wander out. No one was on to him and he had a new jacket, which he sometimes off-loaded to a schoolmate for a few bucks.

Then, after a while, he got requests. Made a fair bit of dough.

By the time Johnny and Jimmy were in their teens, they were on Team Phil. That's what Phil called it.

Jeans and T-shirts. Socks and undies. Whatever. Phil knew how to get rid of it. And the boys had pocket money. Plenty of it.

Then they graduated.

Break and enters. Not much break though.

Around the beaches it didn't need to be. No one locked their doors.

Knock. Knock. 'Hey, Tony!'

If the door was answered, they were told 'No Tony lives here.'

'Stupid bugger's given us the wrong address. Sorry missus.'

On to the house a few doors up. Same play: 'Hey, Tony!'

If no one answers, slip round the back and try the back door. Usually unlocked. If not, on to another.

No breaking down doors. No need.

So now it was TVs, radios, jewellery. You name it. Eventually everything sold.

Phil came from a family of nine. His father and Jimmy and Johnny's dad were brothers.

Jimmy and Johnny were a year apart and always hung out at Phil's. More fun in a house full of kids, with them having no brothers or sisters.

Phil was a dare devil. The two boys gravitated to him. He never bought a train or bus ticket. Bullshitted he'd lost it or something. Always got away with it. Chicks loved him too. In the back row of the picture theatre, kissin some chick while the movie played.

It was an adventure hanging out with Phil.

And then Phil got a licence, even though he didn't have a car; not one he owned. But it wasn't hard to knock one off though. Phil knew how and he showed Jimmy and Johnny.

They'd go on rides to Newcastle or Wollongong, and they'd do a couple houses. 'Hey, Tony!' Same plan.

Leave the car there and nick a new one to get home. Never got caught.

When Phil was twenty, he and the boys knocked off ten surfboards.

The silly owners had stashed them under a fella's place who lived right on the beach. Easier than carting them home. And anyway, who'd knock them off?

Phil, that's who. He knew the owners—blokes he'd sold gear to. He swore to them it wasn't him, but said he'd try to find out who the thieving bastards were.

He sold them to some would-be surfers from the Western Suburbs. They surfed Cronulla, so no way the boards'd be seen around Coogee. Phil got the boys jobs. Concreting, like he did.

Fuckin hard work, shovelling concrete. Still, he had to explain his money away somehow, cos the only other skill he had was thieving.

But it wasn't the thieving put him inside. It was the aggravated assault.

He was cleaning out a house behind the Coogee Bay Hotel one arvo. The two boys were working, but he'd pulled a sickie. Nicked a car.

Found this empty house and was filling a duffel bag when a bloke walked in.

'What the fuck are you doin?'

'Robbin ya,' said Phil.

Then he bashed the bloke with the half-filled duffel with clocks and radios and CDs and videos.

The bloke went down. But Phil was shat off that he'd been interrupted and kept on bashing the bloke.

Then the bloke's two mates came in and bashed the shit out of Phil and rang the cops.

Phil got five years. Three years non-parole.

He kept to himself. Didn't join a gang.

Inside, he had time to think. Not a lot of time to think when you're thieving.

Phil'd always thought his old man was smart, but now he wasn't sure.

His old man had worked on the wharves. Tally clerk. 'A very good job,' as his old man would say.

Had a pen and clipboard and ticked off what was brought in on the ships. Cargo.

And guess what? Sometimes cargo accidentally got broken. Crates fell and were damaged, as was the merchandise inside them.

Meant there were often sunglasses or radios or kettles or clothing brought home in the boot of the old man's car.

Damaged goods. Sure. The old man always had mates down the pub interested in damaged goods.

Phil's old man spent a fair bit of time down the pub.

Too many at home, he'd explain: 'Bloke can't hear himself think.'

Phil'd always thought crime paid, but now he knew it didn't. Big time.

When Jimmy and Johnny came to visit him inside, Phil told the boys: 'Jimmy, Johnny, I steered you wrong and

I feel guilty. I feel responsible. Get a trade—plumber or electrician. You don't want to end up in here.'

'Not us. Don't you worry, Phil.'

'Yeah, Phil, we know what we're doing. Ultra careful.'

Phil begged them to change their ways. Couldn't handle it if they went down: 'Please listen to me.'

And the boys did.

Jimmy became an electrician and Johnny a plumber.

About twelve months into his jail time, Phil was called into the superintendent's office.

'We're putting you in the garden, mate. You shovelled concrete, so now you can shovel dirt.'

Phil didn't mind. In fact, it gave him a new lease on life.

Stopped him thinking and started him reading. About flowers.

All sorts. Especially flowers that liked full sun, because that's what they were going to get at the jail.

Marigolds and snapdragons.

Geraniums and zinnias.

Cornflowers and sunflowers.

And bugger me dead. Phil had a green thumb.

The garden sprouted colours. Orange, white, purple, red, pink, blue and yellow. Sunflowers were definitely his favourite. And boy, could they grow. He had some over twelve feet high. And they were the best yellow. It was like looking at the sun.

The crims were pretty impressed. Gave him some shit like, 'We know where the pansy is in that garden.' Or, 'I'll give ya a bunch of knuckles for a bunch of flowers.' But they liked the garden. Better than the cold hard wall that surrounded them. Way better.

Phil kept reading about flowers. And then one day he asked to see the superintendent.

'Sir, I'd like to build a greenhouse.'

'Why?'

'Cos I'd like to try and grow orchids.'

Phil had to explain to the super how special orchids were. How they had been found all over the world. Even in the Antarctic. There were more than twenty-eight thousand varieties. But they couldn't have the full sun of a Sydney summer on them. They'd die.

Super said he'd think about it.

Well, of course Phil got his greenhouse and the jail got orchids. And it was written about in the *Sydney Morning Herald*. Described Phil as the Orchid Man.

So that's what he became known as: the Orchid Man.

Phil's family visited him inside. Most of them. His mother cried.

His father didn't visit. Said Phil'd brought shame on the name Quigley.

Phil thought, Shame about that. Shame Quigley was such a stupid fuckin name.

His brothers and sisters popped in. Coupla times a year. No one had much to say. Still, nice they put in the effort.

About eighteen months into his time, Phil was called to the visitor's room.

Wasn't expecting anyone.

And there, sitting on a chair at the table, was Maureen.

Phil sat down opposite Maureen.

Phil stared at Maureen.

Maureen stared at Phil. 'Hi.'

'Hi yourself. What are you doing here?'

'In the neighbourhood.'

Phil laughed. 'That's funny.'

'Good. Brighten up your day.'

'Reckon.'

Maureen had lived opposite Phil all his life. She was a coupla years younger, so he'd never paid her much attention. Until he did. When he was around seventeen.

Maureen'd never showed any interest in Phil. And anyway, there were always blokes hanging by her gate on their bikes.

And then a bit later they'd bumped into each other at the cinema.

Sat together.

Kissed a bit.

Groped a bit.

Did it again a couple of times.

But as Phil drifted further into crime, Maureen had drifted away.

'I thought you might like a visit. Heard your old man doesn't come.'

'Nope.'

'Does that upset you?'

'Nope.'

'Do you want me to go?'

Phil looked into Maureen's face.

He'd always liked her face. Sure, she was good-looking. Pretty. But she had a kind face.

'Thanks for coming.' And he smiled.

Maureen came once a month after that, until Phil was released.

Then they got married and moved to the Central Coast about two hours north of Sydney.

———

Terry Reynolds always wanted to be a cop.

Funny that. Didn't have a good reason. No big moment.

So straight after school he joined the force.

When he got through training he knew one thing: don't get sent to the Cross. Kings Cross.

Drugs, gambling, prostitution.

You had to take 'the paper' in the Cross. Paper money. Corruption. Terry didn't want to be a corrupt cop. He wanted to do good.

Terry was stationed on the North Shore. North Sydney, in fact. Opposite side of the harbour to the Cross.

Whew.

He did five years at North Sydney and loved it.

It was community and Terry grew up in community. Bankstown.

His parents' name was Renic. Lebanese. But they figured it wouldn't hurt to Anglo it. So the family became Reynolds. Didn't help much. Still got shit poured on you at school. But it made Terry a very determined man.

And then he was moved to Mosman. Leafy, peaceful, law-abiding, harbourside Mosman.

Not a lot happened in Mosman. There'd be break-ins— mainly crims from the other side. The odd Merc or Jag would get taken for a joyride.

Pretty easy gig for a cop. Mosman was posh.

Kids all went to private schools. The boys were smart-arses and the girls gave lip. They'd be in their bikinis at Balmoral and they'd see you patrolling and come over. 'Officer, I think I've hurt my chest. Could you take a look, please?' Then they'd laugh and run off. Terry got used to it. Everyone grows up different. They'd turn out okay, most of them.

And then He arrived. And all hell broke loose.

Papers called him the Mosman Slasher. He terrorised the North Shore for three years. Brazen. No other word for it. Slashed flyscreens at night and climbed in the bedroom window.

While the woman slept, he would cut her nightie to pieces, sometimes placing it neatly on the end of the bed.

A lot of the time, the husband was sleeping alongside. If the woman woke, he would slash her and race off.

There would be a spike for a couple of months, then nothing for six months. And then up he'd start again.

They found out later he'd been in hundreds of homes. Just watching. Watching them sleep.

But it was the Mosman Slasher who made Terry's name.

Terry decided he was going to catch the bastard. With a couple of his fellow officers they set up stake-outs.

Sometimes Terry would dress in drag and walk the streets at night. The other officers reckoned Terry was too ugly for the Slasher. Reckoned he'd run a mile. But it paid off.

There was a call one night from a terrified young girl around the corner from where Terry was staked out. Someone was trying to get in through her bedroom window. Led to the Slasher running straight into Terry.

That was it.

Arrested for break-and-enter and grievous bodily harm.

The Mosman Slasher got eighteen years and Terry got promoted.

———

She led him through into the lounge room.

She loved her lounge room. Especially the lounge room suite. Pale green. Her son Dennis had won it on a game show on television. It was to do with choosing cards to make up a poker hand. And Dennis won a lounge room suite and gave it to his mum.

'Sit down and have a cuppa before you get started. You do have time, I hope.'

'Always time for a cuppa, Mrs Heslop. Love your lounge.'

She knew he was a lovely fella.

But why was he doing this to her?

She didn't understand.

They were her last two thoughts as she went into a long sleep on the green lounge chair.

Jimmy and Johnny got a van each.

Jimmy the Electrician was painted on both sides of Jimmy's van.

Johnny the Plumber was painted on both sides of Johnny's van.

They got themselves a flat in Coogee and they worked Coogee.

Sure did.

Phil had taught them well. Given them a legit reason to case a place.

'Come on through. Excuse the mess. Don't want the place flooded while we're gone.' Overloading them with info. 'We're off overseas tomorrow.'

'Lucky you.'

Lucky us more like it.

During the next ten years the boys made a killing.

People loved them. Recommended their work. And paid for it big time. Fuck-all left after 'the trip of a lifetime'.

The boys were very professional now. They stuck to the Eastern Suburbs. More money in the Eastern Suburbs.

Stuff they stole didn't get moved in the local anymore. It went up the coast. Down the coast. Interstate.

And then Johnny met Daisy Harris.

Daisy Harris was beautiful.

Johnny fell like a ton of bricks.

They met at a pub. She was with girlfriends, after work on a Friday.

It just happened. It was meant to be.

She was in marketing. Her father had died a few years before and she lived at home with her mum, Betty. At Strathfield, about half an hour west of the CBD.

Johnny and Daisy hit it off. She laughed at his jokes. Found him very funny.

Johnny had never met a girl like her. Sort of sophisticated. Brought up different. Private school, but not up herself.

'What do you do, Johnny?'

'I'm a tradie. Plumber.'

'You'd be very handy to have around I would think.'

'Why? You got a blocked drain? I'll give you a discount. And a lift home.'

Johnny didn't give Daisy a lift home, but he did see her again. She'd given him her number.

They met the next two Fridays, but without the girlfriends.

He loved kissing Daisy. Like velvet.

Couldn't believe Daisy had happened to him. She should have been out of his league.

He picked her up from home one Saturday night.

Crime had delivered Johnny a pretty flash car. Merc. Second-hand, so the cops wouldn't come sniffing, but mickey mouse inside and under the bonnet.

They nearly had it off in the back after dinner. Lot of hands and fumbling, but Daisy wasn't ready and Johnny wasn't going to press his luck.

They arranged to meet the following Saturday.

When Johnny arrived at Daisy's, her mother opened the door: 'Daisy won't be going out tonight, I'm afraid, Johnny.'

'Is she sick, Mrs Harris?'

'No, she isn't, Johnny, and she won't be seeing you again. Sorry.'

And she shut the door.

Johnny stood at the door.

He didn't have a clue what to do.

Eventually he drove home.

Johnny rang Daisy at work on the Monday.

'I'm sorry, Johnny, but I can't see you again.'

'Why?'

'Mum doesn't want me to see you.'

'But why?'

'Sorry, Johnny.' And Daisy hung up.

That bitch.

That *bitch*.

That *fuckin bitch*.

The mother.

That up-herself mother.

A tradie not good enough for her private school daughter.

Right.

Right.

Johnny reckoned there were a lot like Daisy's mum. Up themselves. Jimmy couldn't keep a girlfriend. Went through them like a dope smoker goes through papers.

He knew he was moody. Johnny had told him he was moody.

Can't be up all the time.

Shoulda been, though. He was rolling in moolah.

But he wanted to share the proceeds from his ill-gotten gains.

He bought them all presents.

Flowers.

Maybe it was a bit on the nose giving them underwear on the first date. But hey, girls like saucy underwear. It was advertised in all those mags they buy. Anyway, most of them took the underwear. But when he wanted something in return, they wouldn't come across.

He knew they wanted it.

Forced it on a few.

Said they'd tell the cops, but they didn't.

He knew they wouldn't.

One time he had this date with this good-looking sort from Bronte. They went to a pub down the Quay.

Jimmy was having a good time. Girl was pretty relaxed. All was going well.

Two blokes playing pool. One of them keeps looking across at Jimmy's date.

Jimmy can wear it.

Has a few more beers. Coupla whisky chasers.

Bloke keeps looking.

Jimmy walks over, grabs a spare cue and smashes it into the bloke's face. Breaks his teeth. Everyone is stunned.

'Keep your eyes to yourself, cunt.'

And Jimmy ushers his date out the pub door.

Never saw her again.

She didn't want to know him.

Plenty more fish in the ocean. Jimmy reckoned he could handle anything.

Being an electrician brought a bloke into contact with plenty of lonely housewives. And Jimmy didn't muck around. Any sign of flirting and Jimmy was in like Flynn.

Nadia was a top sort. Would run about in knickers and bra.

''Scuse me, won't you, Jimmy? Running late for lunch with the girls. Can you let yourself out? Oh, but Jimmy, maybe you could pop in tomorrow and change a light bulb for me in the bedroom.' She smiled.

Jimmy smiled. 'Sure thing, Nadia. Not a prob.'

This went on for a few months. Almost once a week a light bulb needed changing.

But Nadia didn't tell Jimmy her husband was a cop.

Detective. Twenty-first division. Those guys didn't fuck around—as he found out.

A knock on Jimmy's door and there the detective is: 'You got two choices, Jimmy. You can keep on shagging my wife, which means you'll be pulled over, licence checked, car searched and questioned about four times a day. Doubt you'll make any appointments. Or you can piss off out of town. And I mean out of town. For good.'

Jimmy told the detective he'd leave town.

The detective hit Jimmy fair in the nose. Broke it.

Jimmy went to see Johnny. Told him the story. Told him they were fucked.

'We do not need a cop hovering.'

Johnny agreed.

They sold their businesses and their vans. Got good money for them. Ten years' worth of clients.

They reckoned it was time to do a Phil. Started looking for places on the Central Coast.

———

It hadn't been easy for Phil and Maureen, setting up after prison.

They found a rent in Gosford. Better chance of finding work there than out on the coast.

Coupla years went by, living pretty frugal. When you've got a record, it follows you round like a bad smell. People are nice, but when they hear you're an ex-crim they're scared off.

Maureen was sure things would turn around.

Phil did some labouring.

Then Maureen got a job in administration in an aged care home. So now they could support a small mortgage.

Phil had enough stashed away from the bad old days to put down a deposit on a weatherboard on Tuggerah Lake.

The weatherboard had once been a corner shop, with live-in quarters upstairs.

Phil tacked a greenhouse to the back of the downstairs and set up a watering system.

'I'm going to plant orchids. Use the shop to sell flowers.'

The shop was still deemed commercial, so no trouble with council.

Maureen was happy as. 'What'll we call it?'

'Dunno. Maybe The Nick. Then whoever comes into the shop is in The Nick with me.'

Maureen laughed. Kissed him big time.

God, he loved Maureen. She'd saved him.

It took a while, but Phil's green thumb kicked in. The Nick started to get a rep as a good place for flowers, especially orchids.

The bloke running it really knew his way around flowers, they reckoned.

Lovely bloke, and only too happy to help with recommendations for your own garden. Would even come out to take a look.

Suggest stuff.

Maureen and Phil had tried for a kid.

Maureen was dead keen.

Phil was happy if that was what Maureen wanted, but coming from a family of nine, he wasn't as gung-ho as she was.

Then they found out Maureen couldn't have kids.

Broke her heart.

Still she was strong.

If that's how it was then so be it. They had each other.

Phil said he'd be happy to adopt if that was what she wanted, but she said no to that. Wanted her own.

But she did lose some of her glow. Just a little.

Years passed.

The Nick was doing bloody well. Phil's rep had spread. Garden centres back in Sydney wanted his flowers, especially his orchids. Being the Orchid Man didn't seem to matter now. Made him exotic, just like his flowers.

Phil hired a young girl to help out, and Maureen left the aged care home and dealt with the shop's finances. Customers got in touch from all over. Eastern Suburbs, Western Suburbs, you name it. Phil was out in the ute delivering two days a week.

'I would like a number of your plants, Mr Quigley, but I'm not sure I can get them home by myself.'

Phil couldn't say no.

'Could you perhaps take a look at my garden and suggest what might grow well there?'

'Don't you worry, love, just jot down your address and phone number in the exercise book on the counter.'

And they did.

Phil wasn't sure he'd get around to them all.

Maureen started to have pains.

Put it down to age. Middle age.

She eventually went to the doctor.

Cancer.

Phil's world crumbled. How could this happen? She was the best woman in the world. Why didn't it get someone else? One of his customers. Phil went to a dark place.

Maureen went to Buddhism. 'Existence is suffering, Phillip. You know that. You came through it. And I will come through this.'

Johnny found a two-bedroom unit with a balcony looking out at the beach at Avoca.

Jimmy found a three-bedroom fibro with a big yard, two streets back from the beach at Wamberal.

They were only a few ks from each other. With the moolah they had buried in different accounts, they could nearly cover the price of each.

There was a bit they'd have to pay off over ten years. Fuck-all really. Cos they knew how to make money. Not a problem.

But getting started wasn't as easy as they thought.

The Central Coast in the nineties was crawling with young families. Everyone had made good money through the eighties and were into renovations. And there were a fair few tradies working the coast. It was a tradies paradise.

But they didn't fancy moving over for a couple of newbies from Sydney.

That was okay for Jimmy and Johnny. They needed to get the lay of the land.

Plenty of time.

And they could duck into Sydney every now and again for a job. Pick up the extra quid.

There was also plenty of fun to be had on the coast. Great nightlife.

The boys were out and about.

Johnny was looking for love.

Not Jimmy. He was looking to change light bulbs.

A leopard never changes its spots.

Only difference now though: Jimmy always asked what the husband did.

Harder for Johnny. No girl ever came up to Daisy.

Fuck, he hated Daisy's mother. Betty fuckin Harris.

He had to stop thinking about her.

Wasn't good for him.

First stop for the boys, of course, was Phil and Maureen.

Maybe they could start Team Phil up again.

But Phil put an end to that idea first up. 'You boys been doin it straight?'

'You bet, Phil,' said Jimmy.

'Straight as,' added Johnny.

They told Phil there'd been no need to thieve when business was so good. 'They were the bad old days, Phil.'

Phil told them Maureen was crook. Real crook. 'You blokes fancy delivering?'

'That'd be great, Phil. Yeah, anything helps. Get to know the area, the people. Work gets work.'

Phil needed to be keeping an eye on Maureen.

The boys understood.

Phil said he'd pay the going rate.

The next eighteen months went pretty good.

The boys made contacts, thanks to the Orchid Man.

New homes going up everywhere and work came their way, slowly but surely.

Maureen's chemo seemed to be working okay but it was knocking her around.

Then middle of the night she took a turn. Told Phil to get her to the hospital.

Phil was holding her hand as she took her last breath. Looked up at him with fear in her eyes. And passed away.

Her suffering had ceased.

Nirvana.

No nirvana for Phil.

———

Terry read through Anne Tierney's file.

Fifty-eight years of age. Two grown children with their own families.

House in Rose Bay had been paid off with the insurance from the death of Ted, her husband.

She'd been found sitting in a lounge-room chair. Strangled.

Whoever did it must have been strong.

No sign of struggle. The room was neat.

Terry looked at the photographs of Anne's neck. The bruises were pretty horrid. Dark. Deep blue.

The file had been sent to him because the Bondi police had come up empty on suspects.

All the neighbours were interviewed. Saw fuck-all.

Happened during the day, pathology said. Between 1 and 2.30 pm.

Anne's bank statements showed up nothing unusual. Her phone was checked for calls, texts. Nothing out of the ordinary.

Not that the ordinary wasn't checked. Cleaners, tradesmen, gardeners, deliveries. All came up zilch.

Terry reached for the second file.

Six months later, Agnes Heslop.

Strangled in her own home. Newcastle. One hundred and fifty ks north from Sydney.

Agnes lived alone. Grown-up family. Unmarried son Dennis. Two married girls, four grandchildren. A husband in aged care. Alzheimer's.

Sang in the choir at St Mary's Catholic church Newcastle. Well liked.

But dead as a dodo now, lying back on her green lounge chair in front of the telly.

Terry put the photo down.

Newcastle police had got nowhere with their inquiries. Nothing.

But a young constable remembered reading about Anne Tierney.

Thought there might be a connection.

And that's how both files ended up on Terry Reynolds's desk. Give it to the cop who nabbed the Mosman Slasher.

See how good he is.

Reckon we might have a serial was what head office thought.

———

Phil was sleeping about two hours a night. If he was lucky.

His fuckin mind was spinning.

Why? Kept going around.

Maureen never hurt anyone.

She so believed in Phil that it made him believe he must be okay. Not the dead-shit fuckin crim that he was.

So it must have been him that caused it.

He'd read about it.

Karma.

Payback for the shit he'd done to people, and what he'd got the boys into. Even though they'd cleaned up their act.

And Phil would cry.

Never cried before.

And it got bad.

Every woman who came into The Nick he could hardly look at.

Why didn't one of them get fuckin cancer? Why were they so fuckin privileged?

Dark, black, fuckin black days.

Phil threw himself into his work. His flowers.

Went to his notebook.

Deliver anywhere. Any time.

He still had the boys helping out. One day a week. Each of them.

They liked delivering, Jimmy said. Get out of the Central Coast. Change the odd light bulb.

———

Terry's first move was to visit the murder scenes.

Both houses had been closed up. Families hadn't sold.

Not easy to sell a murder house. People are sensitive.

Wait a couple years. Everything sells eventually.

Terry tried Anne Tierney's house first.

Always start at the beginning.

Step at a time.

Less chance of missing something. Anything. Small or big.

———

Anne Tierney kept a clean house.

Two bedrooms.

Beds made up.

One room was obviously a guest room.

She had a guest all right. Murdered her.

Forensics had turned up no prints outside the family and cleaners. All of them had alibis.

Simply furnished. Modern. Pastel-coloured walls.

Anne was proud of her home.

Terry liked that.

Reminded him of his mum. Made a home out of a house for him, his sister and old man. Loved adding little things she'd find at markets and vintage shops. Not that she spent a lot. Chose well.

Terry liked to take his own photos of crime scenes.

Took out his phone.

Click. Click.

Moved outside.

Nice garden. Easy-to-look-after shrubs and some flowers. A few in pots.

One pot had an orchid. Purple. Slipper orchid.

Terry was up on orchids.

Mr Johnson had had orchids.

Mr Johnson had lived opposite the Reynolds when Terry was growing up.

People in the street thought Mr Johnson was a bit strange. Always in his greenhouse at the back of the war service home he lived in with Mrs Johnson and their daughters, Lindy and Robin.

Robin gave Terry a hand job once in the back seat of Terry's Valiant after a party at the Johnsons'. Only the one. Never happened again. Never mentioned again.

But Mr Johnson would explain all the different types of orchids to Terry. Terry found it interesting.

Only bloke in the street who ever talked to Terry. After all, Terry was a wog.

When Mr Johnson died, Mrs Johnson had the greenhouse taken down and dumped on the footpath and all the orchids thrown out.

Terry had thought that was a horrible thing to do.

Terry looked at Anne Tierney's slipper orchid, sitting there in direct sunlight.

Slipper orchids need some shade.

Terry moved the orchid under the jacaranda.

Back in the house, Terry sat in the chair where Anne Tierney had been strangled.

He shut his eyes. Let his mind wander over every movement he'd made from when he entered Anne Tierney's home.

Nothing came to him.

Not a bloody thing.

Terry Reynolds stood out front of Agnes Heslop's house.

Terrace in the inner-city suburb of Newcastle called The Hill.

Historical area. Had a prison block there in the early days.

Not now. Bit la-di-da.

Not as la-di-da as Mosman though. What is?

He went inside.

Homey. Another lady who was proud of what she had.

Terry didn't know Agnes's story, but he could tell she was kind. Nothing in the house yelled at you. It wanted to make you feel wanted.

There was the green lounge-room suite where Agnes's life ended. At least it was in a place she loved.

Why kill Agnes?

Files said nothing stolen.

Same with Anne Tierney.

Terry took out his phone and started taking photos.

Went through the house. Room by room. Snapping away.

Had to be something.

Then outside.

Agnes had been quite a gardener.

Lots of trees. Big avocados, one on either side of the yard. Male and female. How else were you going to get a tree full of avocados like Agnes had?

Garden full of flowers.

Pots galore.

Kept snapping.

Then back inside.

Sat in the death chair.

Closed his eyes.

Terry had been given an office at Newcastle Police Station on the corner of Church and Watt.

It was a pretty nice office.

When you're an out-of-towner, you maybe can expect to be given a broom closet out the back. But not here.

And the cops were okay. Anything he needed.

They'd come up blank themselves so wanted this sorted. Not that they expected Terry would turn up anything they hadn't.

It was that time of day. Late arvo, evening coming in. He'd have a beer and a kebab later.

The cops had rented him a one bedroom. Coupla streets behind.

Terry's family was in Lebanon, visiting. Sarah was ex-Beirut. Well, her family was. She came here young, and now she and Terry had young ones. Boy and girl.

And wasn't Sarah on about their education. That's what gives you a chance at life, she reckoned. And a trip to Beirut was part of their education.

He missed them.

Might as well work. He took out his camera. Started looking through the photos.

Bedrooms and bathrooms and backyards.

Gotta be something here.

Gotta be.

He went through them again. Enlarged them.

Agnes's backyard.

Flowers. Pots of flowers.

Pots hiding pots.

And there was a pot he'd missed.

Spider orchid. Green with a nice bit of burgundy.

Just the one.

Like at Anne's.

Just the one orchid.

And both murdered.

Only thing in common.

Wow, are you clutchin at straws?

Maybe it was time for the beer and kebab.

His first phone call was to Anne's son.

Terry knew he'd been questioned inside out at the time of the murder.

Never know, though. He could have forgotten something. Something that Terry might pick up on.

That's why Detective Terry Reynolds had been given the case.

Graeme Tierney hadn't seen his mum for six months, not since he moved to Brisbane.

Anne loved skyping. They skyped Friday evenings.

She did the same with Flora, her daughter.

Even though Flora lived just out of Sydney on the Central Coast. And even though she would often drive to Flora's for the weekend.

Neither thought their mother was a mad gardener. She did what was necessary.

It had been their dad's job to look after the yard while he was alive. Op-shopping was what Anne really loved.

It was Flora who loved gardening, and Anne tagged along willingly while Flora bought plants for the garden.

Agnes Heslop, on the other hand, loved her garden. Always looking for new shrubs and flowers to plant.

However, neither of her children had ever seen her show an interest in orchids. And they had no idea why anyone would want to murder their mother.

Terry woke in the middle of the night. The garbos were emptying bins. Noisy bastards.

He went to the window. Looked down at the noisy bastards.

If neither woman had an interest in orchids, why did they both have them? Why buy them?

Maybe they didn't buy them. Maybe somebody else did.

The murderer.

Terry didn't go back to bed.

He googled 'garden centres'.

There were a fair few garden centres around Newcastle.

Plants R Us was located in The Hill.

'Don't have an Agnes Heslop on the books, Detective. What did she look like?'

He showed Mr Plants R Us a photo of Agnes.

'Nope. Never set eyes on her. Sorry, mate.'

'You sell orchids?'

'Bit exotic for us. Try Let's Go Troppo at Gateshead. They do all sorts of funny shit.'

Gateshead was only about ten ks from Plants R Us, so Terry wheeled on down there.

And yep, Let's Go Troppo sold orchids. But not to Agnes Heslop.

'Never seen the lady.'

'Who else sells orchids?'

'A few others sell 'em but they don't grow their own like us. They get 'em from growers, so they're not always stocked up.'

Terry tried six other garden centres that sold orchids. No one he spoke to had laid eyes on Agnes.

Time to focus on Anne Tierney.

Same result.

Plenty of garden centres around Rose Bay. Eastern Suburbs was flower central. And a couple of places thought they might have seen Anne in their shop. Couldn't be sure. But no Anne Tierney on their books.

Where the fuck did these orchids come from?

Terry went back to the office and closed his eyes.

———

Jimmy and Johnny were having coffee and cake and reading the Sundays out front of the Crowne Plaza hotel at Terrigal.

They both liked it here. Reminded them of Coogee. Sun and surf. And chicks everywhere.

Phil worried them but. Sure, he'd had a lot to deal with, with Maureen dying and everything. Bit hard to get a laugh out of him anymore.

He had been their hero. Taught them about life before his big change after jail and getting married to Maureen.

The boys had liked Maureen. She was sort of straight, but she'd married a crim so you had to give her points for that.

Jimmy folded the paper and slid it across the table to Johnny.

'Big society wedding. Look at that.'

Johnny picked up the paper and read the article. It brought back bad thoughts to him.

Daisy was marrying a toff. Media mogul. He remembered how he'd not been good enough for Mrs Harris's daughter.

Why did Jimmy have to show him the fuckin article?

And didn't Daisy look beautiful. And didn't her bloke look fuckin wealthy. Fuckin big yacht to sail the whatever.

Johnny had to admit it: Daisy landed alright.

Better off with the mogul.

Bet the mother was happy now.

Oh yeah—happy, happy, happy.

All good things come to an end, though. Johnny knew that.

———

Thank fuck for Mr Google. Terry was at the computer.

Miniature orchids.

Orchid societies.

Royal orchids.

The Orchid Place.

Orchid pests and diseases.

Orchid love.

And then, buried deep in Mr Google: the Orchid Man.

A story on ex-criminal Phil Quigley and his shop at Tuggerah on the Central Coast.

Bingo.

Or not.

But a start.

Or not.

'Sorry to bother you again, Flora, but have you ever bought flowers at The Nick on the Central Coast?'

'All the time, Detective. My favourite place for plants. Why?'

'Did Anne ever visit there with you?'

'I guess so. Must have. Yes, sure she did. Why, Detective?'

Detective Terry Reynolds explained 'just following up leads' and hung up.

How good is the light on the New South Wales coast in the middle of winter?

Bloody beautiful.

Bloody clear as.

'Stayin' Alive' by the Bee Gees was playing on the radio as Terry drove down the coast to Tuggerah Lakes.

He remembered seeing a doco on the Bee Gees a few months ago. Brisbane boys. Started their road to fame on *Bandstand*.

The two youngest couldn't have been more than twelve. Barry about sixteen. Robin had big protruding teeth back then. A few million bucks later on fixed those.

Terry drove along the lake.

Great to be alive.

There's that word again.

'And I'm investigating a murder.'

Irony.

Tuggerah Lakes was in fact three interconnected coastal lagoons. Wetlands. Attracting an array of waterbirds.

Terry could see black swans and parrots. There were other birds he didn't know the names of. Bloody lot of birds, though.

The Nick was open.

Wasn't a big joint.

Not like the other garden centres he'd checked out.

Phil Quigley was busy with a customer.

Terry wandered through The Nick.

Pretty sharp.

And definitely orchids.

Reminded him of Mr Johnson.

The customer was taking his time. Rabbiting on.

Finally the customer scribbled something in an exercise book on the front counter. Then he thanked Phil Quigley and left, grabbing a bag of potting mix on his way out the door.

Terry introduced himself.

'I'll need to ask you a few questions.'

'What about?'

'The murder of two women.'

Phil shut up shop and took Terry through into the house.

Terry asked if Phil knew either Anne Tierney or Agnes Heslop.

'Names don't ring a bell.'

Terry passed over photos of the two women.

'Nope.'

'Never seen them?'

'Nope.'

'You'd have a record of all sales, wouldn't you, Mr Quigley?'

'Yep.'

They went back into the shop.

Phil put both names into the computer.

Nothing came up.

'You murdered these two women, didn't you?'

'If you were sure of that, then you'd arrest me. And you're not arresting me, are you? So you can fuck off.'

Detective Terry Reynolds walked to the door. Then stopped.

'What's in the book?' Pointing to the exercise book on the counter.

'Names of customers wanting me to take a look at their gardens.'

'You do that a lot?'

'Sometimes.'

'It's a pretty big exercise book.'

'People like flowers.'

'Especially orchids, eh?'

'Sometimes.'

'I'll need to take a look.'

Detective Terry Reynolds stood at the counter with Phil Quigley and went through the exercise book page by page.

They found Anne Tierney's name.

Then Agnes Heslop.

Their phone numbers and addresses.

Detective Reynolds arrested Phil Quigley for the two murders.

————

Phil could see his garden through the cell window.

He knew there was no way he'd get his old job back.

Twenty years in solitary.

Maybe down the line things would change and he'd be allowed out into the yard for a few hours.

Maybe then he'd ask if he could work in the garden.

It was doing okay. But nothing like when he had it.

Just flowers and shrubs.

No orchids.

The trial was pretty quick.

Why not? Phil had pleaded guilty.

There was some stuff in the papers about him being the Orchid Man and his previous sentencing.

Some said he should never have been allowed out. That might be right.

Phil was okay with this.

He deserved it.

Karma.

————

He knocked on the front door, just like he'd done with the others.

She opened the door.

She was an old woman now.

'Yes? Can I help you?'

She didn't know who he was.

'Hi, Mrs Harris, it's me—Johnny. I used to go out with Daisy a few years back.'

'O yes, yes. Well, Daisy doesn't live here anymore.'

'Yes I know that, Mrs Harris. I read about the big society wedding Daisy had to that media mogul. It was in all the papers.'

Mrs Harris stared at him.

'You must have been thrilled. I was so happy for Daisy and I was in the neighbourhood and I work with flowers now. Have my own business. Doing very well. And I thought why not pop in and leave a present for Daisy? An orchid.'

He held the orchid out to Mrs Harris.

'Oh, how beautiful. What a lovely yellow.'

'It's a moth orchid. Grew it myself.'

Mrs Harris smiled up at him. 'Well, why don't you bring it inside and I'll put on a cup of tea. You can look through the wedding photos.'

'I'd love that.'

And he followed Mrs Harris into the house.

'You sit here on the lounge and I'll put the kettle on.'

He sat with the wedding album, looking at photo after photo of the Eastern Suburbs cunt that had married Daisy.

He had no doubt that Mrs Harris would have been very pleased with this match.

They sat opposite each other drinking tea.

Then he got up and leant over Mrs Harris.

Betty Harris wondered what he was doing as he put his hands around her throat and ended her life.

Just as he had ended the lives of Anne and Agnes.

He took the Moth Orchid and placed it on the sideboard in front of the lounge-room window.

He knew it would need bright indirect light to grow properly.

He had learnt a lot about orchids since delivering for Phil.

Then he wiped away any trace of his visit.

When he was done, he left the house, walked a couple of blocks to where his van was parked, and drove north.

THE TEA-LEAF

Sam was a tea-leaf.

Nature or nurture? He'd read all that shit. But just cos his great-great-great-grandfather came out as a convict for nickin, didn't mean Sam would have nickin in his blood.

Sam just liked nickin. Anything. It'd always been like that. Shoplifting oranges and lollies from the greengrocer's on the way home from school. And even at school he'd had a gang of shoplifters by the time he was fifteen.

They stole a camera from the chemist shop by the station. The camera was tied down with six cords and every day one of the gang would undo a cord until the camera was free of cords. Then Sam just walked in and lifted it into his school bag while another of the gang got the chemist's attention.

Easy. Sold it to a kid at school who got too much pocket money.

That's when Sam first got called a tea-leaf by a pommy migrant. Rhyming slang. Tea-leaf. Thief.

And then after school it was break-and-enters and cars and any bloody thing. Not banks or big stuff; just easy stuff.

Loved it. Never got caught. Too careful.

But now. Fuck. This was scary.

All Sam was doing was avoiding a bloody long walk home.

Should have got a new car battery. He'd known it was on its way out, like every other bit of the car. But hey: if it works, keep it.

Got the bus down to the pub, but when he was leaving there were no buses. So he had to toe it.

Well, not toe it, but walk it, anyway.

Two ks and a bit pissed.

Just wanted to be home in bed.

And then this wanker just up ahead dives out of his car and races to the front door and a bloke answers, and they go inside, and Sam notices as he passes that the keys are in the ignition.

And it's a Volvo. V40. Top line.

So Sam jumps in and takes off as the bloke comes out, yelling to him to stop.

Too late. Sam turns the corner and he's out of sight of the bloke.

Drives to near home. Few doors down from his flat.

Gets out of the car and then, like the good tea-leaf he is, he decides to check the boot. Never know your luck.

Fuck! The boot is full.

The boot is full of coke.

Not cola. Fucking cocaine. Packets of it. Bundles of it. Worth a bomb.

Well, smart thing to do would be to leave it. Don't want Mr Big on your back. He'll kill you for stealing his cocaine.

But Sam can't look a gift horse in the mouth.

He races upstairs, grabs a couple of duffel bags and fills them. Then he drags them upstairs.

Takes about twenty minutes and no one's around to see it all happen.

Once he's finished, Sam races to his window, where he has a clear view of the street.

Watches for about an hour.

No one comes. They probably expect the car to be miles away by now.

Next morning the car's still there.

Sam thinks this through.

Then he rings the cops from a public phone. 'Bloke drove up last night, parked his car and then ran off. Not sure, but I have a feeling it's stolen.'

He gives the cop the address of the car, but won't give them his name when they ask. 'Don't want to get involved. Just trying to be a good citizen, officer.'

And then he rings off.

Back to his room and the view from the window.

About an hour and a half later the cops turn up. Two of them. Look in the car. Open the boot.

Then they knock on a few doors. No one knows anything. They don't come to Sam's flat.

Then they leave.

Sam rings the NRMA and tells them about his battery. Says he probably needs a new battery. Doesn't take long for the NRMA to arrive and change the battery. Bloody good, the NRMA.

The car is still out front.

Late afternoon the two cops are back with a bloke. It's the wanker Sam saw with the car the night before. The three of them stand around talking. Then the cops take off.

The wanker watches them disappear, then goes to the boot and opens it.

Boy is he surprised.

And he's shitting himself, Sam reckons.

The wanker takes out his phone and makes a call, all the time looking around. Then he hangs up and gets into the car.

Sam races down to his car and follows the Volvo, keeping his distance.

———

Garry Tierney loves driving for Nick Latoof. Nick is a very big shot. Has his finger in a lot of pies but mainly drugs.

Has a great house in Campbelltown. Campbelltown is in the western suburbs. South-west of Sydney. About an hour and a quarter drive. Used to be country but not anymore. Houses as far as the eye can see.

Garry reckons Nick's his meal ticket to a great life. Lots of money, lots of girls.

But now. Fuck. This is bad.

He only stopped for a sec to see Bobby, his best mate, and tell him he'd see him at the club later. Had a job to do first: deliver Nick's coke.

Then that stupid cunt stole his car. The Volvo V40 and the coke.

Had to have known about the coke. Must've been following him. Then they transferred it to another car obviously.

When the cops knock on Garry's door the next day, he nearly shits himself. They say his car has been reported stolen.

Describe the Volvo. Ask if it's his. The cops don't say anything about the coke.

Garry doesn't know what to answer. Takes the plunge. 'No, officer, my car is parked outside, where I left it last night.'

'Show us.'

Garry walks outside and feigns surprise when his car is nowhere to be seen.

'Come with us, Mr Tierney. We know where your car is.'

Garry still isn't sure they haven't found the coke. But there's his car.

Cops hand over the key and tell him to take better care of his car. 'Not a good idea to leave the keys in the ignition.'

Garry says that's what comes from driving home pissed.

They tell him to come down to the station later and fill out a report. Then they drive off.

Garry can't wait to get to the boot.

And nothing.

No coke.

Can't have been the cops. Has to be another outfit.

But what the fuck will he tell Nick?

———

Sergeant Aaron Gray has been a cop for twenty-five years. Always stationed near his home in the western suburbs.

He could have retired after twenty years. Most cops do.

The stress. Huge.

But Aaron loves his work.

Maybe he loves it more because he is a Jew. There aren't many Jewish cops in Sydney. Not out here anyhow.

His father and mother came out to Australia after the Second World War. Migrated from Shanghai, which was one of the only places to accept Jews at the time.

America didn't.

England didn't.

Australia didn't.

His old man opened a deli in Bankstown. Everyone said it was a stupid idea, but it wasn't. He did well.

And then in the seventies the family moved to Campbelltown. This time Aaron's father opened a couple of delis. Again, he did pretty good.

But Aaron didn't want to work a deli. Too quiet. So he became a cop.

And that isn't quiet in Campbelltown.

Lots of good people in Campbelltown. Salt of the earth. But there are also real evil bastards.

The drug dealers. They never cared who they got hooked. The more the better. Didn't matter what age.

The vulnerable kids were those with shitty parents. You could feel sorry for most of those shitty parents, seeing as they probably had shitty parents too. But you couldn't always feel sorry for the kids. No siree. Most of them had been given every chance. After the war their parents worked hard. But their kids got lazy. Got pissed and watched TV. All day.

What chance did these kids have? Out there looking for a family. Other kids like themselves. So they discovered drugs.

Aaron got on well with most people. What most people didn't realise was that he was smart. Knew the only way to catch the evil bastards was to have the inside on what was going on. Informers. Blokes and girls he'd caught for naughties. Became their friend. 'Let you off this time, but I may need your help at times. Okay?'

'Yeah, sure, Sarge.'

And a deal was sealed.

And so this car was now supposedly stolen. An anonymous caller who didn't want to give his name. Had to be someone who lived nearby. Taken it as a lark.

But something smells rotten.

'What you reckon that was about, George?'

George is the constable who went to check out the car with him.

'Dunno. What d' you reckon, Sarge?'

'We'll see. Won't we, constable?'

Nick Latoof is not happy.

His big bad boy Alex took Garry down to the cellar under Nick's great house in Campbelltown and beat him up.

They know how to do it, these enforcers. The guts. The face.

It hurt, but Garry is just pleased he's still alive. Now he sits on a chair in front of Nick.

'Let's go over it again, eh, Garry?'

And Garry does. Tells Nick everything, same as he did earlier.

Exactly the same. No lies. Not worth it.

'And again, Garry.'

So Garry does it again.

'Alright. So what do we do now, that's the question. Any ideas, Garry?'

Garry doesn't have any. He hurts too much.

'Two choices, the way I see it,' says Nick. 'One: it's a competitor. But who the fuck? Two: some fucker has come across it by accident and thinks all his Christmases have come at once. You'd better hope it's number two, Garry.' Nick stares at Garry then shakes his head. 'Get him a glass of water, Alex.'

And Alex does.

Nick is convinced whoever stole Garry's car now has Nick's cocaine. Either a conspiracy or a cock-up, but most likely a cock-up.

Doorknock the street it was dumped in. And the surrounding streets, if you have to. That's Nick's plan.

Garry walks to the counter at Campbelltown Police Station.

One of the constables he'd talked to before is on duty. 'Here, fill this out.'

And the constable hands Garry a form. 'Trip over, did you? Fall down the stairs?'

'How'd you know?'

'Having a bit of trouble understanding you through that busted lip. Speak up.'

Garry starts filling out the form.

'Often leave your keys in the ignition?'

'Couple of times.' Garry hands back the form.

The constable looks it over. 'Where'd you say you'd been drinking?'

'At a mate's.'

'What were you doing there?'

'Nothin much. Just yackin. Watchin the telly.'

'Yeah? What's your mate's name?'

'Hold on. I'm the one that's been robbed. I'm the victim here.'

The constable laughs. 'Your mate's name and address. Write it down.'

Garry does.

Garry gets in his car and takes off.

Pulls up a bit later.

Rings Bobby. Knew he'd be at work.

'Bobby. Garry. If the cops ask, I was at your place drinking till late, okay?'

'What time?'

'Around midnight. Thanks, mate.'

Garry rings off.

———

The constable and Sergeant Gray are having a cup of tea in the police station kitchen.

'Definitely a beating?' asks the sarge.

'No doubt. Must've hurt.'

'So why does our Garry get a beating for having his car stolen?'

'Maybe something in it, Sarge?'

'Guess there must have been, Constable.'

The Sarge looks at the report. 'Let's pay Bobby a visit.'

___

Nick Latoof sits in his leather upholstered armchair behind his mahogany red desk in his wood-panelled office in his great house in Campbelltown.

He's sweating.

He's down one hundred and twenty kilos of cocaine. Street value at least two and a half mill.

He bought it from the Arab for a mill. That's half a mill down and the other half a mill due after he's off-loaded it. He's getting a mill and a half from the Greek on delivery. But the problem is the Greek has already paid a deposit of half a mill. That was the half mill Nick paid the Arab. So Nick is now deep in the shit. He still owes the Arab a half mill and he's into the Greek for a half mill. And he has no cocaine to get him out of the shit.

Nick rings the Greek. Says there'd been a hold-up. Just a couple of days, that's all. It's not a problem, he tells the Greek.

'No, it's not a problem, Nick. Not for me. I get my coke or you get dead. Two days.' Then the Greek hangs up.

Nick rings the Arab. 'Just a hold-up in transfer. Only be a couple of days. You know how it is.'

'No, Nick, I only know how it has to be. You owe me half a mill. Two days or you be dead, Nick.' Then the Arab hangs up.

___

Bobby is a motor mechanic. He works at Camden Motor Repairs. Camden is on the outskirts of Campbelltown.

Bobby likes working with his hands. He's known how to take a motor apart and put it back together since he was fifteen years old.

His old man taught him. He was good, the old man.

Croatian. Straight-up hard worker. Instilled that in all the kids. Bobby's sister is a lawyer. Smartest one in the family.

Bobby's boss is a good bloke. Pays fair. And overtime. Not like some of the bastards who'd squeeze blood out of you if they could. Bobby likes his job, so he's unhappy when the boss brings Sergeant Gray over to see him.

Sergeant Gray introduces Bobby to the constable and says they just want a bit of info on his mate Garry Tierney.

'Sure. Garry not in trouble, is he?'

'Hope not, Bobby. Did you see Garry yesterday?'

'Sure, he came over in the evening.'

'What for?'

'Just for a drink and a chat. We're good mates. Hang out together. Talk bullshit. Get pissed.'

'What time did he leave?'

'Had to kick him out around midnight. I had work to do today.'

'How'd he get home, Bobby?'

'Had his car.'

'Driving pissed, was he?'

'None of my business, Sarge.'

'Garry says you watched some telly. What was on, Bobby?'

'Buggered if I can remember. On in the background.'

'Can't remember anything, Bobby?'

'Bit too pissed I guess.'

'Lucky you weren't driving, eh, Bobby?'

'Never drink and drive, Constable. Might hurt someone.'

'Good boy, Bobby. Don't want to get in trouble with the law again.'

'No, Sarge.'

'If you think there's something I should know about last night that's slipped your memory, you know I'd appreciate it.'

Bobby nods, and the sarge and the constable turn and leave.

Bobby knows Garry was on a delivery when he stopped by. And he knows what the delivery was, cos Garry works for Nick Latoof.

And everyone knows what Nick does for a living. That's how he got that great house in Campbelltown.

———

Sam is sitting on his bed, staring at one hundred and twenty kilos of cocaine.

One bag he can get rid of at the pub easily enough. But trying to shift more bags that way, word would get out and Sam would be mince. As in meat.

And he doesn't fancy that. He's small fry.

He needs help.

And then there is a knock on the door.

Sam throws a rug over the coke, closes the bedroom door and opens the front door.

Two blokes are standing there. One is big, and the other is the wanker who owned the car Sam nicked. But he looks different. Like a bus has run over him.

'Hi, my car was stolen last night and someone reported it to the cops. I just wanted to thank the person who reported it. Meant a lot to me. Wish there were more people like that, looking out for each other. Bloody Christian thing to do. Was it you, mate?'

'Me? No, mate. Don't know nothing about it. Bloody good tho. Definitely Christian thing to do.

'Me, I'm an atheist. Mum and Dad were Seventh-day Adventists. Pretty strict. Glad to get away from it.

'Anyway, you don't want to hear about that. Sorry I can't help.'

The two blokes stand there at the door.

Then the big bloke speaks. 'You keep your ears open for us, eh? Might be something in it for ya. Here's a number to contact us on.'

And the big bloke hands Sam a card with a mobile number on it. Nothing else, just a typed number. 'What's your name, mate?' he asks.

'Sam. Yeah, sure. Will do. I'll keep the ears cocked.'

And then the two blokes turn and walk up the stairs to the next flat, and Sam closes his door.

Sam leans against the back of the front door.

He's fucked.

That big bloke would of killed him.

Shit.

What to do with the fuckin cocaine?

———

The Arab was born in Australia. Parents were Syrian, migrated here in the early eighties.

He never liked school. Well, learning that is. School learning.

But it was at school the Arab learnt he was a trader. That's what he'd picked up from his old man. Buy. Sell. Simple. Find something someone wants. Get it for a good price and then sell it on for a better price.

Sometimes the Arab didn't even need to have the product he was selling. Tell someone you had what they wanted, get a deposit and then go look for it. If you were any good, you'd get the product for the deposit and wham-bam the rest was profit.

At Lidcombe High School every kid had wanted weed. So the Arab found a supplier and became a seller. Or a drug dealer, as the media liked to call it.

Great place, Oz. Capitalist country. Land of opportunity.

But the other important thing when you were a trader was: don't let anyone try to pull a swiftie on you. Be tougher than the next bloke.

So the Arab needs to send Nick a message.

He has Nick's pride-and-joy Maserati set alight. One of his boys drops a Molotov cocktail onto the front seat while it's sitting in Nick's drive.

Boom.

Noisy, but noise sends a message.

By the time the fire brigade gets to Nick's, the Maserati is a burnt-out wreck.

Nick will pay attention. He owes the Arab a half a mill.

The Greek's grandparents came to Australia after the Second World War. So many Greeks came over, they reckon Melbourne is the second-largest Greek city after Athens.

But the Greek headed north to Sydney after he finished high school. His parents were still in Melbourne, but the Greek's father's cousin Alessandro had a greengrocer's shop in Marrickville and a job for the Greek.

The markets in Sydney opened at 4.30 am, so that's when Alessandro expected the Greek to be there buying the fresh fruit and vegetables for the shop. And the Greek was good. Knew what to buy.

Knew how to get the best price too. Hang in there. Be funny. Win them.

Then, after a few years of early market work, the Greek found a better product. Weed from Griffith in country New South Wales. Truckloads of it came in. The Greek saw it was the future.

But now he was out of weed, and into cocaine.

A lot of blokes were getting into methamphetamines now. Making a motza. But not the Greek. He had kids. Didn't like the thought of kids getting hooked on that stuff. No future in that. A little coke, though? That was different. And still good money.

And now Nick Latoof has a problem supplying the Greek with his cocaine, when the Greek has already laid out half a mill. Nick needs a lesson. Just to sharpen him up. Let him know you don't fuck with the Greek.

So the Greek has one of his boys blow up Nick's wife's Merc while it's sitting in the car park at Campbelltown Mall. Reckons Nick will get the message.

———

Nick is getting a lot of messages, and now he has the cops on his doorstep.

They're all over the Maserati. The Merc had been towed to a depot.

Why would someone want to do this to Nick and his family? Sergeant Gray wants to know.

And of course Nick has no answer. 'I'm a law-abiding fella, officer. Pay my taxes. Send my kids to a good school. Donate to the Lebanese Muslim Association. Keep the young kids engaged in worthwhile pursuits. Law-abiding, officer.'

Sergeant Gray and the constable go back to the station and write out a report. But Sergeant Gray smells something.

Twenty-four hours after a car that must have been holding something was nicked, there's a bombing of two cars belonging to a known drug dealer.

Sergeant Gray smiles as he reads over his report.

By the time the wanker and his very large companion come out from knocking on every door in his building, Sam is sitting in his car, waiting.

He watches as they go in and out of every house in the street. And the next street. And then they drive off.

And Sam follows. To a great big house in Campbelltown.

Sam waits.

Hour later the wanker comes out and gets into his car and drives off. To his home presumably. Sam follows.

Pretty old block of flats. Jerry built in the sixties, like everything.

Someone made a big quid in the sixties. Probably a lot of someones.

Lights go on in an upstairs flat. Behind a tattered blind, Sam can make out the wanker at the sink.

Now Nick is getting it from his wife.

'What the fuck, Nick? It was brand-spanking fucking-new. Two fucking weeks old. And now it's a fucking burnt-out fucking wreck.'

Nick is sitting behind his mahogany red desk. He doesn't feel well.

'So what are you going to do about it, Mr Big Man, eh? You gonna just sit here and let whoever did this get away with it? With bombing my Merc.

'My Merc which I loved.

'Which was a birthday present.

'Which all my girlfriends were envious of.

'What are you going to do about it, Nick?'

And then she started bawling.

Nick's wife Sarah weeps a flood. And Nick asks himself the same question. What is he going to do about it? And about the bombing of his own car. His Maserati.

But Nick is a practical man. He has to be.

His wife isn't practical. She's ruled by her emotions.

Things are bad enough now. He'd better get it sorted before Sarah does something stupid. Like stab him.

So he organises to see the Arab and puts a proposition to him.

'You give me another hundred and twenty kilos and I put my house up as security. I owe you five hundred K now, which takes it to one point five mill. The house is worth over two point five mill. If I don't get you the one point five in a month, you get to sell my place and take your money.'

'Sounds okay, Nick, but there's been a little change.

'Cost is now one point two mill for a hundred and twenty kilos. So you'll owe me one point seven mill in a month.

That's still covered by the house, though, so it's sweet by me. Sweet by you, Nick?'

Nick wants to bash the Arab's head in, but Nick is a practical man. If it all goes to shit, he still has eight hundred K equity in the house.

'Sweet.'

'Good. We'll prepare all the paperwork.'

When Nick gets home Sarah is beside herself with happiness. She grabs him and plants kisses all over him, then drags him into the bedroom.

Amazing what a new Merc will do. Hopefully he will be able to pay for it.

Of course he'll be able to pay for it. Next big deal and he'll be back in front.

He knows what he's doing. And when he finds the missing hundred and twenty kilos, he'll be laughing.

Next Nick goes to see the Greek at his warehouse in the industrial estate on Blaxland Road.

Nick and the Greek go into the Greek's office. They tell their gorillas to stay outside.

Nick apologises for the delay. Can't trust anyone these days. But everything's okay now and he has the coke. On delivery, all the Greek has to do is pay the mill that's owing.

'That's good, Nick, but you fucked me around and I don't like being fucked around. So here's the deal.

'You deliver the hundred and twenty kilos to me here tomorrow night at eight sharp. And I'll be giving you eight hundred K, not a mill.'

'Hey,' says Nick, 'the deal's a mill on delivery. You know that.'

'I know the deal's changed, Nick. It wasn't here when it was meant to be. That put me out with a number of my suppliers. I don't like to be out with my suppliers. Gives me a bad name.

'Eight hundred K to you tomorrow night on delivery of a hundred and twenty kilos of powder to me. Okay, Nick?'

Now Nick wants to smash the Greek's head in, but instead he counts to ten inside his own head then says, 'Okay. Tomorrow night at eight.'

When Nick gets back to his office in his great house in Campbelltown, he sits behind his red mahogany desk and does the sums. His scribbles show he's now nine hundred K short for the Arab.

Plenty of equity in the house. But getting fuckin less all the time.

Bloke needs to be a fuckin mathematician to keep up.

———

Sergeant Gray and the constable knock on the door of Garry's flat.

Garry opens the door. 'Shit, what have I done now, Sarge?'

'Dunno, Garry, what *have* you done? We just need to ask you a few more questions. Okay if we come in?'

The sarge and the constable sit on the lounge. It's covered in magazines, which they move aside.

'Like to read, eh, Garry?'

'Yeah. A bit.'

Garry stands at the sink.

'Not sitting down, Garry?'

'No thanks, Sarge. Like it up here. Healthier.'

'Into health, eh, Garry?'

'Isn't everyone these days?'

'Drinking a lot of piss don't seem healthy to me, Garry.'

'Bloke needs a bit of fun every now and again, Sarge.'

'Yeah, you're right, Garry. That's what we wanted to talk to you about. The bit of fun you had with Bobby the other night.'

'Told ya everything I could remember, Sarge.'

'Said you were watching television, Garry. Remember what was on?'

'Jesus, how'd you expect me to remember that? We were yackin on the whole time.'

'State of Origin, Garry?'

'Good try, Constable, but that's not until next week. I remember now. It was that weird film, the one with the Australian actor all painted blue. *Avatar,* isn't it?'

'Yeah, wild movie. Watched it myself.'

Sergeant Gray looks at the constable then to Garry. 'Who you working for, Garry?'

'Different blokes. All sorts of jobs. Bit of driving. Labouring sometimes. Whatever gets me a quid.'

'All legal I hope, Garry?'

'Course, Sarge.'

'You know Nick Latoof lost two cars yesterday, Garry?'

'What d'ya mean lost? Nicked like mine?'

'Nope. Blown sky high. A Maserati and a Merc. Nice cars once. Who do you think would do that, Garry?'

'Fucked if I know, Sarge.'

'You know Nick, don't you, Garry?'

'Only a little bit. Done the odd job for him. Driving him around, you know.'

'Nothing illegal I hope, Garry? Like not carrying stuff you shouldn't?'

'Course not, Sarge.'

Then the sergeant and the constable get up from the lounge and walk to the door.

'Things are hottin' up in the old Campbelltown, Garry. You hear anything, you get in touch, mate, alright? We'd really appreciate it.'

Sergeant Gray and the constable open the door of Garry's flat and walk out, closing the door behind them.

About an hour later, there's another knock on the door of Garry's flat.

Garry opens the door. He's seen the face before.

'I've got your coke. Can I come in?'

Garry remembers; it's the bloke from the block of flats he and Alex doorknocked, and he's struggling with two big duffel bags.

'Don't know what you're talking about, but you can come in.'

'I'm Sam, remember?'

'Yep. Now what's this bullshit you're going on about?'

'Mind if I sit down?'

And Sam sits on the lounge, which is still warm from the cops, and dumps the duffel bags on the floor.

'I got your coke. And let's not play games. You know what I'm talking about.

'White stuff. Bags of it. Kilos of it.

'You shove it up your nose.

People pay a lot for it.'

Garry goes to the fridge. Opens it. Takes out a beer. 'You want a beer?'

'Don't mind if I do, ta.'

Garry hands Sam a beer. Twist top. 'Okay. So if you reckon you got my coke then you must also have figured out it's not mine. It belongs to someone you should be very afraid of.'

'The bloke who bashed your face?'

'What d'ya want, Sam?'

'It seems to me like we both got a similar problem: a bootload of coke.'

'And why is that my problem?'

'Because, Garry, if I get caught with it, mister, whoever owns the fuckin coke is gonna reckon you had a part in it getting taken.'

'And why is that?'

'Because that's what I'm gonna say, Gaz, old mate.'

Garry sits and stares at Sam.

'We have to find a way to get rid of this stuff,' Sam says, 'and I need your help. We can't just dump it. It will be found and that will lead back to you and then to me. We are in this together, bro, whether we like it or not.'

At that moment Garry's phone rings.

It's Nick Latoof.

Garry nearly shits himself. What the fuck's going on?

Nick tells Garry he needs him again. Same deal as before. Pick up at the Arab's and then on to the Greek's.

Garry has to be at Nick's at 7 pm tomorrow.

This time Nick will be travelling with Garry.

Sam and Garry sit on the lounge.

They are very quiet.

Then Garry rings Bobby. Asks him to come over.

'It'll have to be after work, Garry. Couple hours.'

Sam and Garry wait.

'Want another beer?'

'May as well.'

Garry gets them both a beer, then he sits back down on the lounge.

'Want to see the coke?' Sam asks.

'May as well.'

Sam undoes the duffel bags and empties the coke onto the floor.

'Lot of bloody coke.'

'Yep. A fuckin lot, Garry.'

Bobby arrives at 5.30 pm.

Garry introduces Sam.

The boys have covered the coke with a blanket.

'Beer?'

'Thanks.'

Garry hands Bobby a beer.

'So what's this about?' asks Bobby.

Garry pulls the blanket away.

'Holy shit. That what I think it is?'

Then Garry explains the situation.

'So you didn't know what was in the boot when you nicked the car, Sam?' asks Bobby.

'Nope. Just after a ride home.'

'Bobby, we got to get rid of it,' says Garry. 'You gotta help me.'

'Help you sell it? No way. This has got nothing to do with me, Garry.'

'No, I mean we need to dump it where it will never be found again. You must know places where shit gets dumped. Like old cars and stuff. Buried. Never to be seen again.'

Bobby sits down on the lounge. He stares at the bundles of coke.

Then Garry explains the plan. If the stolen coke disappears, no one will be able to point the finger at either Garry or Sam.

And now Nick has sorted out a new deal and he and Garry are picking it up from the Arab tomorrow night and delivering it to the Greek's warehouse after.

'So then everything will be hunky-dory. But I need you to get rid of this shit. Please, Bobby.'

Bobby looks at the coke, then at Garry, then at Sam, then back to the coke.

'Yeah, I'll help you, Garry. What are mates for?'

'Yeah, what are mates for? I knew I could count on you, Bobby.'

The boys help Bobby load the duffel bags into Bobby's car.

Then Bobby takes Garry aside. 'Gaz, I'm happy to help, but you got to promise me you'll leave this sort of caper behind from now on. No more involvement with drug dealers.'

'Promise.'

Then Garry hugs Bobby.

———

Garry doesn't sleep well that night.

Nor does Sam.

Or Nick.

The Arab does.

The Greek does.

Bobby does.

And so does Sergeant Aaron Gray.

And Sarah. She keeps dreaming about her new Merc.

Garry arrives at Nick Latoof's place at six o'clock. He can tell Nick is nervous.

Garry hasn't seen Nick like this before. Nick's a big shot.

They go into Nick's wood-panelled office, where Nick sits on his leather-upholstered chair.

He rests his arms on his mahogany red desk.

'We can't fuck this up, Garry. Your car in good nick?'

'You betcha, Nick. Best car in Campbelltown. You know that. Volvo V40.'

Garry loves his Volvo. Nearly died when it was stolen. He'd stashed money aside for years to buy a top-line car.

Got lucky. The car's only ten years old.

His dad was a driver. Limos for a hire car company. First job he got when he brought the family out from Scotland.

Hated being called a ten-pound pom. He was a ten-pound Scot. And he reckoned Volvos were the best.

Paul McCartney had a Volvo. Garry's dad's best mate had worked security for McCartney and he drove a Volvo too, a station wagon.

But Garry was never gonna be a limo driver. Better money to be made driving for the boys. The big bad boys.

Like Nick Latoof. Who now pulls a gun out of the drawer of his mahogany desk.

Garry freezes.

'Just in case, Garry. You stay in the car at all times, and if I say go, you gun it. Right?'

'Right, Nick.'

Garry's legs are shaking.

He's scared.

———

The Volvo V40 pulls up out front of the Arab's.

One of the Arab's boys comes over to the car. 'The lawyer's here. Needs you to sign some papers. Then fuck-knuckle here and his tin can need to drive round the back for a load-up.'

Nick gets out of the Volvo and goes into the house.

He's never been inside before. The house is cool.

The main room is like a big tent with carpets everywhere, even hanging from the sides of the tent, and wild-looking cushions on the carpeted floor.

The Arab sits on a throne at the back of the tent. He wears robes. There's tea boiling on a small gas stove.

Nick thinks he's in a movie.

A bloke in a Bulldogs rugby league jumper and shorts and thongs stands alongside the Arab.

'This is God,' says the Arab. 'He handles legals. Sign this.'

God hands Nick a piece of paper and a biro.

Nick reads the contract. It's what they've agreed on. 'Looks fine.' And then he signs. 'Won't need to use this, though, cos I'll have your dough within the month.'

'Good.'

Then the Arab gets up out of the throne. 'Let's load up.'

And they do, into the boot of the Volvo that Garry has driven around to the back of the house.

'A throne.'

'What?'

'Fuckin Arab was sitting on a throne.'

'A *throne* throne?'

'Yeah, a fuckin throne. Like the queen has. Like made out of ivory or something. And bloody gold stripes all over it. And huge feathers coming up the back of it. Peacock feathers, I reckon. And bloody large statues of lions on both sides. He's fuckin mad, I tell ya.'

'Wouldn't have been ivory. Would've been bone.'

'How the fuck would you know, Garry?'

'Not easy to get ivory these days. Costs a bomb. And it's illegal.'

'We're talking about the Arab. He's a criminal, Garry. Think he cares if it's illegal?'

'Still reckon it'd be bone.'

'How would you know about thrones?'

'Read about them once.'

'Where?'

'*National Geographic*.'

'Where would you get *National Geographic*, Garry?'

'I subscribe.'

'Fuck me dead.'

And Garry and Nick drive on in the Volvo V40 for their meeting at 8 pm with the Greek.

It's 7.58 pm when the Volvo V40 approaches the Greek's warehouse off Blaxland Road.

'Pull up bit before.'

Garry does. Keeps the car idling.

Nick has a good look around, then takes his gun out from under the seat.

There are two gorillas standing by the warehouse. Iron shutters cover the opening to the building. Garry doesn't feel good.

Nick tucks the gun into the back of his pants.

'Looks alright, eh, Nick?'

Tony doesn't answer.

'Okay, drive in.'

Garry moves away from the kerb. The entrance to the warehouse compound is a couple of hundred metres along from where they were stopped. There's a high iron-mesh fence surrounding it and a closed gate.

When the Volvo V40 drives up to the gate one of the gorillas undoes the chain securing it and waves the Volvo through.

'Go on through to the front of the warehouse, mate.'

The gorilla closes the gate and follows the Volvo to the warehouse, where the shutters are lifted and Garry is waved inside by the second gorilla.

Garry drives in and stops. He keeps the engine running. Plenty of room here. There are just two Mercs parked inside, with the Greek standing next to them along with another gorilla.

The Greek walks over to the Volvo. Bends down to talk to Nick.

'Good to see you, Nick. Nice and punctual. I like that.'

One of the gorillas asks the Greek if he should bring down the shutters.

'No need. This'll be over before it starts, won't it, Nick?

'Tell your boy scout to turn off the engine. Bad for the environment, carbon dioxide.'

Nick looks to Garry and nods. Garry turns off the engine.

Nick gets out. Shakes hands with the Greek. 'Got your goods.'

'Got your eight hundred K. Let's get down to business.'

'How we do this?'

'You show me yours, Nick, and I'll show you mine.'

Couple of the gorillas laugh.

The Greek then gives the order for one of his gorillas to open the boot of one of the Mercs.

Nick tells Garry to do the same with the Volvo's boot.

The Merc's boot is laden with cash. All hundred-dollar notes.

Eight hundred thousand dollars takes up a lot of room.

Then Garry steps aside. The Volvo's boot is laden with coke.

'Okay, let's exchange,' the Greek says.

And then it's all hands on deck as the coke is transferred into the boot of the second Merc and the cash is transferred to the back seat of the Volvo.

'We may as well have a beer to celebrate, Nick. Let's step into my office.'

And the Greek turns and walks a couple of metres into a room with a table, sink and fridge.

As Nick turns to follow, Sergeant Aaron Gray, his constable and two other cops barge in from a side door.

'Hands in the air! Now! You're all under arrest.'

Nick goes for his gun and is immediately shot in the shoulder. He crashes to the ground.

The three gorillas dive behind the Volvo, but quickly give themselves up when three shots slam into the Volvo.

Garry screams and shits himself.

The Greek, meanwhile, is standing in the office with his hands in the air and a smile on his face.

'Hello, officers. How can I help you?'

———

Sarah is dancing with girlfriends at the Ivy, a Sydney hotspot, when the phone call comes through.

She has to shout over the noise.

'What did you say? Speak up.'

And they do, telling her that Nick is being held by the cops.

She doesn't ask 'what for' because she doesn't really care. Nick is turning into a fuckwit. And anyway, she has a new Merc and a great house in Campbelltown.

Sarah ends the call and she and her girlfriends dance the night away.

———

Next day, Sergeant Gray goes to speak to Nick.

Nick is in hospital under armed guard. They'd operated on his shoulder. He'll live.

Sergeant Gray tells Nick he's in big trouble. He's been arrested for dealing in a large quantity of drugs and is facing a fair few years in the big house. He's also being charged with possession of an unlicensed firearm.

'Care to make a statement, Nick? Might help.'

———

The Greek and his gorillas were taken to Long Bay prison. They'll be tried for dealing in drugs.

The Greek wasn't too unhappy about that. Goes with the game. With good lawyers and a guilty plea, he'll be back in the game in a couple of years.

But he is fuckin psychotic and ready to fuckin kill Nick Latoof.

Down one point three million bucks and a hundred twenty kilos of powder, thanks to that arsehole. Nick doesn't have much time left on the planet if the Greek has anything to do with it—and the Greek will definitely have something to do with it.

The Arab hears about the bust. Everyone does. It's front-page news and all over the TV.

He knows that Nick will not be making good on what he owes him: a cool one point seven million bucks.

But how cool is the Arab? He smiles. He has a lien over Nick's house for the one point seven. It will fall due in a month.

'Good to do business with you, Nick.'

Garry is charged as an accessory. He's released on bail.

He can't work it out. He thought he'd be up shit creek without a paddle.

The sergeant tells him not to leave town. Campbelltown. He tells Garry to sit tight.

Sergeant Aaron Gray is getting all sorts of compliments from the department. Even if there was a bit of 'nose out of joint' from the Drug Squad, who reckoned he should have notified them.

But the sarge just says, 'There was no time,' and 'I had to move fast.' Eight hundred thousand dollars of dirty drug money and two hundred and forty kilos of coke.

Course, the media is only told about the hundred and twenty kilos at the warehouse.

Sergeant Gray will announce the discovery of the other hundred and twenty kilos in a day or two. Say it was found dumped.

Got to look after your informers.

Sergeant Aaron Gray is looking at a promotion.

———

Garry drops around to Bobby's after work. They have a beer.

Garry goes through the whole thing, brings Bobby up to date on all the moves.

Says it was pretty exciting, but he was never scared. Was fuckin terrible what happened to the Volvo but, hey, he's alive.

Says it was such a surprise when the cops arrived. 'How did they know?'

'Smarter than we give 'em credit for, Gaz.'

Bobby and Garry have another couple of beers and settle down to watch the State of Origin.

———

Sarah opens the door of Nick's great house to find two detectives standing on the doorstep.

They introduce themselves and inform Sarah that the police are impounding the house and the Merc.

'What for? You can't do that!'

'Sorry, ma'am, proceeds of crime. You'll have to move out.'

'When?'

'Now.'

And then the flood starts.

But floods don't last long with Sarah.

A month later she's sharing an apartment with Ahmad. He owns a gym at Bankstown. He's on the straight and narrow, Ahmad. Good businessman too. There are always blokes coming to the apartment to get their vitamin supplements.

Sarah isn't with a fuckwit now.

———

God is standing by the throne, telling the Arab the bad news.

'Can't sell the house. Cops got it.'

The Arab looks at God. 'Make sure Nick meets some of my friends while he's inside.'

God makes a phone call.

———

Sam is sitting looking out the window, contemplating life.

He thinks he might move north. Gold Coast. Bit hot down here in Campbelltown.

Might get a nice flat overlooking the beach at Southport.
Could easily pay six months in advance and a bond.

He goes into the lounge room. Sits on the lounge.

On the table in front of him are three bundles of powder.
They'll pay for the rent and bond.

About sixty grand there, maybe more if he does it careful.

Must've rolled under his bed while they were loading.
Nobody did bother to count.

What do they say?

'Once a tea-leaf, always a tea-leaf.'

Sam thinks that's pretty funny.

A TIME TO DO

Frank Testy was shaped by his name. 'Testy is as Testy does,' they would say at the Institute. Back fifty years, Frank had won the national 100 yards breaststroke championship title, but he'd been a bit over the Olympic qualifying time, so no Munich for Frank.

Instead he'd turned to coaching, which he liked and was good at. He became head swim coach at the Australian Institute of Sport during the late eighties. Discipline was his mantra. No discipline, no good. Didn't matter how bloody talented you were, you were fucked without discipline.

Coaching served him pretty well. Saw the world, paid the bills, bought him a house at Bondi and gave him a life with Mary.

But Mary died five years ago and Frank got lonely.

And here he was now, swimming from South Bondi to North Bondi and back to South Bondi. Long deep strokes, a breath on the sixth stroke. Freedom. Or it should be.

That's what his lawyer had said when he'd come to tell him he and five others were being released.

But he's not free. Because it keeps going around in his head. 'Who? Who did this to me?'

Oh yeah, he knows Sue May set him up. Set him up big time. But who was behind it?

And why wouldn't Frank have helped Sue May? She'd been great. Brought him out of himself. Made him laugh, made him care.

Sexy too. That was it, wasn't it? The sex. Yeah, a beautiful sexy forty-year-old had fallen for Frank Testy. What a stupid prick. What price ego? A huge fucking price, it seems now.

'Lovely Asian lady looking for long-term relationship with sensitive man. Likes music, dancing and walking in beautiful scenery.' Couldn't hurt to reply, so he did. And that started it.

Phone conversations with plenty of laughter. And didn't Frank need that.

The weekend she'd booked and paid for at a Sydney hotel. Couldn't let her pay, though. Sent the money to her straight away. But her mother, who lived nearby, got ill and she had to cancel.

It was terrible how her sisters wouldn't help. It all fell on Sue May.

Frank was able to lighten the load. Lightened it quite a bit. What good was money to him with no Mary to spend it on?

And then their planned trip to Hong Kong. Only for the weekend. To see her father.

Sue May had come to Bondi. Fucked him senseless and convinced him.

Of course, at the last minute Sue May couldn't go. Mum had got worse. But Frank should go. Dad was expecting him and she had presents for her father.

So he went and Dad May was a good bloke. They spent Saturday and Sunday together and at the airport Monday morning, when saying goodbye, Dad May produced a package for Sue May.

Soap and incense? Sure, I'll just shove it in my bag. Not a problem.

Not until Hong Kong customs wanted a word.

Not soap and incense. Heroin. Five kilos.

And no Dad May to be seen, and no Sue May on a number that was no longer connected.

Just a dirty fuckin prison cell for four months.

In the end, the judge said they were all stupid but not mules. Not drug mules.

It had been all over Hong Kong television, and then all over the world. The six of them having a celebratory dinner on their release.

But to celebrate what? That he had been made a fool of? That he had just spent four months in that fucking disgusting sewer with four hundred pieces of shit?

And then he came home.

But no one wants to know him. They all seem to think that where there's smoke, there's fire. They all think he's a drug mule, and a druggie as well, probably.

He has been a member of the Bondi Icebergs for twenty-five years, since he and Mary first moved to Bondi. Yet two weeks he's been back and not one decent 'Hi, Frank. You doing okay?' Not an anything.

And he knows them all. Fuck, he's been on committees, he's donated, he's brought swimming champions to fund-raisers and he's outswum all of them through the years.

Swimming doesn't exhaust Frank, but he is tired.

Treading water now, he looks back at Bondi, at the beach, at Campbell Parade. At the suburbs beyond, where she must have lived. But he never got to see her joint. Always next time.

Why not just swim down. Down as far as possible. Down there, he wouldn't have to think about it.

Or why not stay here, treading water. For how long? Into the night, if necessary. Plenty of bull sharks around Sydney beaches. One of them would sniff him out eventually.

Frank thinks about it.

And then he turns and continues his swim.

Long, deep strokes, a breath on every sixth stroke.

Friday night and Frank Testy has been sitting, watching television for the past two hours. And there's not one fucking thing he can remember about it.

Staring at the television is what he's been doing. Staring and staring and staring.

He knows there's drinks on at the Icebergs tonight for the members. And he knows he'll be treated like a leper if he turns up.

But Tony McGee will be there. Him and his beautiful Asian girlfriend, Lee. She's nice. She always smiles and waves at Frank.

And Tony is okay too. But he has been pretty distant with Frank since you-know-what.

Haven't they all? I guess those commercial pilots think their shit doesn't stink.

Stop being such a fuckwit, Frank. Tony might be able to help.

Frank Testy walks through the door and goes straight to the bar.

Then he takes his beer onto the balcony and looks out into the night over the ocean.

God he loves the ocean. The smell. The power.

He turns to look inside, through the window.

Yep, they're all there.

Tom, the race starter, and Bill Gower, who's in charge now. Always wanted to be the boss did Bill. Doesn't do a bad job.

And Bill's missus. Mary and her could talk all night.

Maybe it's me. Maybe I haven't said g'day. Maybe I feel guilty.

Feel guilty for chasing skirt. But Mary's been dead five years.

And there's Tony coming in now with Lee.

Frank takes his drink inside and walks up to Tony and Lee as they leave the bar.

'Hi, Frank,' says Tony.

'Hi, Frank,' says Lee.

'Tony! Lee!'

Bite the bullet, you silly bastard.

And he does and asks Tony if they can have a talk.

Frank's figured that if he can get the passenger list for his flight home—or the one he should've come home on—then someone on that flight might have seen him at the airport with Dad May, or have taken a photo, or who knows what. Anyway, he has to start somewhere.

But Tony says he can't help. 'Everyone's moved on, Frank. I'm a dinosaur like you. Wouldn't have a clue who could get me the list.'

'Tony, you were a fuckin Qantas pilot, for fuck's sake. Qantas pilots are gods. You must be able to get that list.'

'Darling, you must try to help Frank. He's been through so much. Please, darling.'

Thank God for Lee.

Frank watches as she leans in to Tony and gives him a kiss. Frank can taste the kiss. How he wants it. And how he hates the thought.

'Mate, I don't like my chances, but leave it with me.

Maybe someone up there still likes me. Never know. You want another?'

Tony goes into the bar.

Frank sits looking out to the ocean.

He looks down as Lee places her hand on his. Lee tells him that Hong Kong is a bad place with bad people. She knows. It's where her parents fled to with her during the Cultural Revolution.

'Tony will help you, Frank. He's a good friend.'

And Tony does help.

A call from Lee two days later tells him Tony has a list.

Three hundred and fifty-three names and their contact details.

'Hi, my name is Frank Testy. I was booked on QF 128 from Hong Kong to Sydney on the twenty-ninth of January this year.'

Always silence.

'I know you were also on that flight and I wondered if you might be able to help me.'

And pretty well it was always the same: 'Mr Testy, I know exactly who you are and I have no intention of helping you with anything. Please don't call me again or try to contact me.'

Sometimes that's followed with: 'You are scum, Mr Testy. They should have kept you locked up and thrown away the key.'

And then they hang up.

But they don't know Frank Testy.

Get the noes out of the way and eventually there'll be a yes. It might take a hundred calls or two hundred, but Frank knows. It's a matter of statistics. His salesman father had taught him that. He sold insurance.

And sure enough: 'Mr Testy, it was terrible what happened to you. I felt so bad for you. I could see in your face that you weren't a bad man. How can I help?'

Even so, Frank is tongue-tied. He nearly bursts out crying. And he hasn't done that since Mary's funeral, when he'd bawled like a baby and couldn't stop. Had to leave the funeral.

'Mrs O'Connor, I . . .'

'Jean, Mr Testy. Can I call you Frank?'

Frank explains that he is wondering if Jean saw him at the Hong Kong airport. If she'd noticed a man with him.

He tells her that he is determined to find out who had set him up. That he doesn't really know how he'll find the bastard, but he has to give it a try.

Jean says she doesn't think she can help, because she hadn't noticed Frank at the airport. He thanks her and is about to hang up when she asks if photos would help.

She had been in Hong Kong to see her son play rugby against a Hong Kong college side. It was a great game and her son's team had won. At the airport all the boys had been snapping away. The competing Hong Kong side had farewelled them and had also been taking photos and videos on their phones.

The conversation ends with Jean promising to ring back after she has collected everyone's photos.

'I won't tell them what it's really for, Frank. Some might not want to help. I'll tell them I'm making up something special to commemorate the trip.'

Frank stops there. He figures he couldn't ask for more than what Jean has promised.

What he would see he didn't know, but it was a start.

He felt excited.

Like when one of the kids he coached has swum a personal best.

Frank Testy walks into Professor Leong's office. This is his third visit.

The Australian Federal Police had suggested he talk to someone. It would help with the trauma he'd suffered.

Frank doesn't know about this trauma business. He's been a fool, he knows that, but every decision had been his.

He is not going to be a victim.

But that's what he is.

Fuck.

'How are you doing, Frank?'

At least the professor asks, even if he is being paid to. And he is being paid a lot.

Not as much as the bloke who came to fix the dishwasher and was there for twenty-five minutes. This is an hour and the professor is going to fix his trauma.

'So-so,' Frank replies.

'Sleeping?'

'You know, on and off. Except last night it was mostly on.'

'Go on.'

And Frank tells him about Jean and the photos and videos, and how they might help him track down the cunt who fucked up his life.

And maybe that made him sleep better. Something positive going on in his mind or brain or subconscious or whatever.

'And why are you doing this, Frank?'

Silence.

Silence.

Silence.

'And why are you doing this, Frank?'

'I'll tell you why, Professor. Because I train people who want the impossible. I convince them that they can achieve the impossible. And you know what, Professor? Some of them fucking do achieve the impossible.'

'So you think it's impossible, what you are trying to do, Frank? Do you want revenge?'

'Yes. I want revenge.'

Frank has always wondered why the professor's office is so sterile. Sort of like a swimming pool. He feels quite comfortable here.

'Thursday fortnight, same time, Frank. Let me know twenty-four hours in advance if you can't make it and we will make another time.'

Frank does a swim.

When Frank is swimming, he's in total control.

Sure, something could happen—a shark, a boat, a heart attack. But the water can't beat him. It's where he belongs. He is secure in the ocean.

Frank dries off in the Icebergs.

On his way out, he bumps into Lee. She wonders if Tony's list has been any help.

Frank tells her about Jean. Stacks of photos and videos. He can't wait to get a look.

Lee is excited for him. She is glad Tony could help.

It's Saturday morning.

Frank likes Saturdays. Everyone comes to Bondi.

Upstairs at the North Bondi RSL on a Saturday morning means a coffee and the papers. And a view of the beach.

Why is Bondi such a great beach? It's the shape, isn't it? Something so beautiful about the shape and the rocks and the northern headland.

Nothing in the papers.

Everyone is an expert. Everyone has an opinion. No knowledge, just an opinion that they know is right.

What happened to bumping into life and learning from it? Real knowledge.

And now some Sudanese fucker has got himself killed, leaving a wife and two kids. Drug related, they say. Something to do with a drug syndicate. Out there in the suburbs.

Frank looks at the bloke's face. Good-looking bloke, he thinks.

Another fool.

Two days later Frank Testy receives a FedEx package. On the back it says it's from Jean O'Connor.

Inside he finds a rectangular red plastic object. It's flat.

Frank knows this is called a hard drive. And he knows what's on it.

There is a note with the hard drive. Jean tells him that she compiled a bunch of stuff. There are fifteen videos and two hundred and five photos. She hopes it helps and says to call if there is more she can do.

Frank plugs the hard drive into his computer and a folder comes up.

The photos are pretty useless. Just kids pulling faces and hugging each other. Not much background in any of them.

Frank works his way through the videos. Kids can be total fuckwits. That's why you like being around them. Silly as.

There's one video of a bunch of them coming into the airport from the footpath. They're yelling and shouting.

All vying for attention. But in the background there is Dad May standing by his car.

Frank pauses the frame. Dad May is shaking hands with someone. A black man.

Frank stares. Then he gets up and searches the bin for Saturday's paper. Fuck, where is it?

Fuck, fuck, fuck, where did I put it?

He races outside to the blue bin for recycling paper and cardboard. He almost dives into the bin. And there it is.

He brings the paper back inside. He places it alongside the paused video. And it is. It's the same face.

The face of the Sudanese bloke killed in the Western Suburbs of Sydney. The bloke they believe was killed because of drugs.

Frank is calm.

He checks the name of the dead Sudanese against the list of people on the flight to Sydney.

And the name is there: Michael Ondine.

Frank goes down to Bondi.

He starts swimming. Long deep strokes, a breath on every sixth stroke.

Bonnie Testy was born two and a half years after Frank and Mary were married. For Frank it was perfect, like doing a personal best.

There was his love for Mary, which nearly broke his heart every time he thought of her.

He had never known you could feel this way. All the time. Every minute.

And now Bonnie. He thought he would burst with love, if that was possible.

That's what he would think every time he looked out at the Pacific Ocean, where he could see forever.

Bonnie got anorexia nervosa when she was fourteen.

Some of the girls Frank trained struggled with eating disorders. Most of them gave up the swimming. Frank felt for them, but mainly he was sorry they would never reach their potential. A couple could have made the Olympics.

Bonnie swam.

She was good.

Was in the water at six months with Frank by her side.

She loved the water.

She cleaned up at school carnivals and then was in Frank's training squad at the Icebergs. He knew she would never be a champion, but he didn't tell her that.

Bonnie trained hard. She got fourth in the nationals at twelve. But she wanted to do better so she trained harder. Lost some weight, reckoned that would get her a few tenths faster. Trained around the clock.

Frank told her to slow down, but she didn't. She was obsessive about what she would eat and wouldn't eat.

When Bonnie wasn't training she would retreat to her room. That worried Frank, because his Bonnie used to love to sit around and yak.

And then she really started to lose weight. Life went out of her eyes and she looked pale.

His Bonnie was never pale. She loved to feel the sun on her body. She wasn't stupid, like some kids; she wore a hat and covered herself in sunscreen. She would have a go at Frank if he didn't wear a hat.

But now she was pale.

Frank tried to talk to her but he wasn't good at it. At the Institute they had psychologists to help the kids. Frank was no psychologist.

They went to see a doctor.

Anorexia nervosa.

It took until she was twenty for Bonnie to get on top of it. To get well.

Frank blamed himself. He shouldn't have pushed her with the swimming.

Mary said it wasn't that. She told Frank he was the best father going, but not everything goes to plan.

And then Mary died.

Frank worried that Bonnie would go under. But Bonnie became the strong one. When Frank fell apart, Bonnie looked after him. Got him back on track. That's how he knew she loved him.

So what does Frank do?

Gets caught up in a scam for dirty old fucking useless pricks like Frank.

And now Bonnie doesn't want to know him.

She says she hates him. Says he never really loved Mary, or he wouldn't have got caught up.

Says she thinks he was smuggling drugs and deserves to be hated by everyone.

She won't see him. Won't answer the phone.

Frank found out the same thing happened to most of the other five who were arrested in Hong Kong.

They went home and found out they didn't belong.

Kids, husbands, wives didn't want to know. Didn't believe them.

Another reason to find the bastard who did this.

There are about thirty people at the funeral. It's held out west at the end of the suburbs, at a cemetery Frank knows.

Many years ago his mother had bought a plot here for when she died. Said she didn't want to burden them all with the cost of her passing.

When Frank and his mum and dad came out one weekend to look at her plot, the whole place was pretty barren. Only a few plots had been used.

Frank's mum was a little worried because the plot near her had a headstone with an Italian name on it. She was worried the bloke there mightn't speak English. But one further along stated that that bloke had been a flautist with the Sydney Symphony Orchestra. That made her feel better. She said they'd have something in common. Frank's mum played piano.

But today is Michael Ondine's funeral and the cemetery has changed a lot in forty years. There are graves everywhere and trees too.

Strange what happens to the suburbs.

At first they come in, cut down all the trees and build loads of houses. It's bloody hot growing up at that time. And then, years later, it's all leafy and different.

He sees there are a number of Sudanese. Mostly Sudanese. A sprinkling of Anglos.

Why are you here, Frank? he asks himself.

The question should be: what the fuck do you think you're going to achieve for fuck's sake? You're a swimming coach. Not a fucking cop.

But he tells himself: I need to talk to his wife. That might give me something. I don't know, but I got to try. For Mary. For Bonnie. For fuckin me, fuckin me. Okay?

'Hi, Frank.'

Frank turns to see a woman he's never laid eyes on before. She's white, about forty-five and not unattractive.

'I'm Jean. Jean O'Connor. I sent you the photos.'

Frank is lost for words. It's all going strange.

'What are you doing here?' he says before he can stop himself.

Frank wishes he'd said something more intelligent, like, 'Oh, hi, Jean. This is a coincidence.' But eventually he would have had to ask the question: 'What are you doing here?'

Jean tells him that Michael was a helper at the House of Friendship, where she volunteers. It's an old convent where refugees congregate to learn English and gain skills to help them move into the community.

They do cooking classes and all sorts of things. In fact, Michael's wife began a small catering business with some of the other women.

Their first job was for Jean's son's school. They catered the send-off party for the rugby team before they left for Hong Kong.

It's because of his wife's involvement that Michael was asked by the school if he'd be available to go with the boys to Hong Kong; the school was short of an adult chaperone.

Jean says it's terrible how Michael was killed. The whole Sudanese community is in shock. Michael was widely liked, but there are bad people around who prey on refugees, knowing they need money.

'They are very vulnerable,' Jean says. 'Why are you here, Frank?'

Frank looks into Jean's eyes, which are warm and honest. 'I need to talk to Michael's wife,' he says.

Mrs Nula Ondine lives with her two kids in a two-bedroom brick cottage in the western suburbs. The garden is tidy. The inside of the house is clean. This house means something to the Ondines.

'Mrs Ondine, I understand this is a difficult and painful time for you and your children. I don't want to add to that. But I think the evil people who killed your husband are the same people who have ruined my life. I would like to ask you a few questions. Do you think you could cope with that?'

Jean O'Connor has convinced Nula to see Frank. At first it was a definite no, but Jean is pretty good at getting her way. Nula trusts Jean. Frank has to make sure he doesn't wreck that trust.

'Mr Testy, I already talk with the police. I tell them I don't know any stuff. Michael a good man. He look after me and children. That all he care about. I not able to help you.'

Frank isn't sure where to go with his questions. Isn't sure what questions to ask.

But he was a swimming coach and that had taught him to get every stroke perfect before you moved on. And above all to be logical.

'Mrs Ondine, where is Michael's phone?'

Nula replies that Michael never had a phone.

'I have a phone,' she tells him.

'Where is it now?'

'The police have it.'

'When you and Michael were not together and you needed to contact each other, how did you do that?'

'He ring me from House of Friendship.'

Frank looked at her. She began to sob. The boy and girl ran to her, and she hugged them.

Whatever they had gone through to get to Australia was probably horrific, and now they had to somehow cope with this.

Frank's problem seemed very small.

'I'm sorry to have upset you, Mrs Ondine. Thank you for your time. I'll see myself out.'

Frank Testy walked to the door and, as he began to open it, the sobbing stopped.

He looked back at Nula Ondine. She was drying her sobs with a white handkerchief.

She looked up at Frank.

'Sometimes he used his friend's phone.'

There were three of them, Frank guessed, and they hurt him. They didn't break anything but they belted the shit out of him.

He was opening the front door, his mind filled with Nula Ondine.

One grabbed him around the throat while another picked up his legs and charged into the house with him. A third slammed the front door closed behind them.

Once inside he was thrown onto a chair. A nylon rope was wrapped around his arms and a pillowcase tugged over his head.

He saw nothing.

He could feel the panic rise.

Get the breathing right. That's what Frank thought. That's what he did.

Deep and slow. In between whacks. Not easy. Concentrate.

They picked him up off the floor and slammed him back onto the chair.

One spoke. He sounded Asian, but Frank couldn't be sure.

'You will be killed if we come again, Mr Testy. This is not a game. Be glad you are alive.'

And then he was belted across the face and ended up on the floor.

The door slammed and Frank blacked out.

It's not easy swimming when you're battered and bruised. But what else is Frank to do?

Long deep strokes, a breath on the sixth stroke.

Frank remembers being beaten up in a pub in the inner city. It was his twenty-fifth birthday and he was drunk. His mates had given him a green cowboy shirt, which he wore to the pub.

There was a bit of a disagreement over whose turn it was on the dartboard and Frank didn't like the way one bloke came on.

Big mouth. So Frank told him where to go.

The bloke took Frank apart.

Blood all over his new shirt.

Great birthday present.

At the time Frank was seeing a French girl who worked as a chef at the local sports club. When she saw Frank and his beat-up face, she wasn't turned off. She was turned on. 'My little mafia' she called him.

What had surprised Frank was how quick the face heals. End of a week and new as.

Frank has been trailing Clinton Hanifa for three days now.

After his beating, Frank had thought long and hard. How much of a fuckwit was he? Those blokes weren't just a few smart-arses. They were crims. Heavy fucking crims. They would kill him. He knew that.

So Frank made a phone call.

Bonnie didn't pick up. She still hated Frank.

And now he is parked by the side of the track, almost hidden, spying on Clinton and two of his mates. Sudanese too, he reckoned.

They are mucking about on the edge of the river. Playing around like kids, splashing each other and wrestling. Not going too far in. Not swimmers.

Nula Ondine had given him Clinton's address. Not far from her. Just around the corner.

Clinton works at a garden centre three days a week and puts in some time at the House of Friendship. He also helps Nula with the kids.

Nula had told Frank that Michael and Clinton were like brothers.

The first couple of days Frank had just watched. But today the boys had headed to the river.

So had Frank.

Frank strips off. Always wears his speedos. Habit. Never know when the water will call.

Frank jumps in, swims about. Clinton and his mates take no notice.

Then the other two take off but Clinton stays, stretching out on a towel.

How good is Oz.

Suddenly Clinton is off his towel and in the water. How did that happen?

Frank has grabbed him while he dozed and hurled him into the river. Frank is surprised at what a strong bastard he still is, given his age. Must be the swimming. Makes you strong.

Clinton tries to say something as he struggles to get back to the bank but Frank keeps pushing him back, further back, until Clinton can only just touch the bottom.

And then he can't.

That's when the panic starts.

Frank gets behind Clinton, grabs him around the neck and strokes further out.

It's deep out here.

Frank tells Clinton he wants to know about Michael. Who had set him up with the drug blokes?

Clinton doesn't know anything. Nothing. That was all Michael's stuff.

So Frank let Clinton go.

And Clinton sinks.

And then splashes up.

And sinks.

And splashes up, screaming.

Frank grabs him around the neck again.

'Not nice, drowning, is it, Clinton? In the papers tomorrow it will say young Sudanese man found drowned in Cooks River. Clinton Hanifa. No suspicious circumstances.'

And Clinton begs for that not to happen.

But it is gonna cost him.

———

Bonnie loves the seagulls.

She loves how white they are.

She loves that they are scavengers.

Throw one a chip and then there are twenty, thirty, all wanting chips.

Some people hate that, but not Bonnie. She'd grown up with it. That's just how they are. You got to survive.

Bonnie is finishing up her fish and chips on the balcony at the Icebergs.

She'd been coming here forever. Waves and seagulls and surfers.

And weed. This is where she scores.

She smiles thinking about what Frank would say if he knew.

Maybe she should tell him. That would teach him.

Bonnie doesn't want to hate Frank, but he deserves it.

Her mother has only been gone a little while and now this: sex and drugs.

Fuckwit.

The quiet young man slips her a bag and takes off with his two fifty. Maybe she'll blow a joint and feed the seagulls down at the park.

'Hi, Bonnie.'

Tony McGee and Lee sit down beside her.

They don't ask first and that annoys Bonnie. What is it with these old people? Think they own the world.

'How's Frank?'

Bonnie looks at them both. She wonders where Tony had found Lee.

She has to fight the bitterness that is taking over. Why had her father done it? He doesn't need someone to replace Mary. He has Bonnie, who loves him to bits.

She feels the emotion rising in her, but she isn't going to break down in front of these two.

'Dunno, haven't seen him.'

'We're worried about him. If you see him, will you tell him that?'

'Sure. If you'll excuse me, I'm just on my way out. Gonna feed the seagulls.'

Tony McGee and Lee watched Bonnie go up the stairs, heading outside into the hot Sydney sun.

———

Clinton Hanifa had been helpful.

A bit.

Michael Ondine had received calls on Clinton's phone, but no numbers were listed. And Michael only ever called Nula on Clinton's phone. But Michael did make calls on the House of Friendship phone. Clinton had noticed that.

Frank speaks to Jean O'Connor.

'I need to know who Michael phoned, Jean, please. Can you search through the numbers on the last phone bill and let me know of any that don't appear to be connected to the House of Friendship?'

Jean does as he asks. There are a lot of unfamiliar phone numbers listed on the bill.

'Frank, I'm not worried about myself, but the House of Friendship is very important.'

Frank was unsure now. He's been beaten up, after all.

He tells her, 'It's your call, Jean. Whatever you decide.'

That evening he gets a phone call from Jean. She gives him three numbers.

Frank uses the phone out the front of the Bondi Hotel on Campbell Parade. He has no intention of using his own phone and winding up dead in the water.

The two mobiles are duds. Nothing. No ring tone. Nothing. Probably in a garbage bin somewhere. Frank has seen *The Wire*.

But the third number is answered. It belongs to a Korean barbecue restaurant in Campsie.

Campsie is ten ks west of the city and is pretty much an Asian suburb now. Used to be real Anglo. You wouldn't want to hang around Campsie on a Friday night in the seventies. Get a smack in the mouth for breathing in Campsie in those days.

But now, great little restaurants. Korean, Chinese, Vietnamese. Fresh fish for sale, and fruit and vegetable shops all down the main street. Beamish Avenue.

And people. Lots of people. Asian.

Frank apologises, says he's got the wrong number and rings off.

'I wouldn't call this a date, Frank.'

Jean and Frank are sitting at a bus stop opposite the Yum Yum Korean Barbecue Restaurant.

'And you look a bit silly with those teeth.'

Frank had rung Jean and asked if she fancied lunch.

Jean asked if it was a date.

Frank said yes.

He'd lied.

He went to a toy shop and bought some stupid false teeth. And some thick-rimmed glasses. And a beanie.

He isn't taking any chances.

Frank should have been seeing Professor Leong today. It's Thursday. He's meant to ring if he can't make it.

But Frank doesn't give a shit. Navel-gazing isn't his thing.

Probably have the Federal Police on his back now: 'It will be good for you, Frank, after what you've been through.'

How the fuck would they know what he'd been through?

No more gazing. Time to do. That's what Frank reckons.

Sitting beside Jean at the bus stop, watching the hustle and bustle of Beamish Street, Frank can't work out why all the young Asian women are so beautiful. The place is swimming in them.

Or is he just getting old?

Is it because he is now in the shadow that he notices attractive women? They don't notice him; he understands that. But what's with him?

He was a lay-down misère for Sue May. Easy as.

God, he misses Mary.

Just falling asleep at night with her by his side made him happy. Getting her a cup of tea in the morning made him happy. She was his companion. You have to work at that. He did.

And then she was gone.

And now he's staring at these other women.

Frank turns to Jean. Jean is attractive. Jean is helping him. With his revenge.

'The massage parlour is popular, Frank,' she says.

Frank has noticed. 'Yep.'

The entrance is next to the Yum Yum, but the massage rooms are above the restaurant.

'I'm hungry, Frank. You promised me lunch.'

Frank smiles. Jean is pretty cool.

So they get up, cross the road and enter the Yum Yum.

———

Clinton Hanifa makes a phone call.

He is scared.

The swimming man scared him. A bit.

But the drug men scare him a lot.

He had lied to the swimming man. Clinton says it was only Michael who did stuff.

But so did he.

And now he had helped the swimming man.

Clinton is scared and confused.

Michael shouldn't be dead. That was wrong. Michael was his friend.

But Clinton doesn't want to die like Michael, so he makes a call.

Tells the lady what had happened.

———

'The rice keeps getting caught in my teeth.'

'Of course it does, Frank. What do you expect with those teeth?'

Jean and Frank have ordered lunch.

Frank loves pork belly. Jean is a vego. Frank doesn't get vegos. It's like something is missing from the plate.

Diet had become a big deal at the Institute over the years. But Frank reckons you need plenty of protein to swim fast, and you don't get enough of it from vegetables.

He knows he might be wrong on that. But that's what he reckons.

Anyhow, the Yum Yum is nothing special. Formica tables and aluminium chairs. Clean, like all Asian restaurants. Efficient, like all Asian restaurants.

A counter at the entrance and a woman behind it. Jean and Frank are told to sit anywhere they please.

The restaurant is pretty full. A fair few Anglos and Middle Easterns eating. Staff from the bank and the imaging centre opposite, he guesses.

The kitchen is down the back of the restaurant. A couple of blokes working it. And there's a stairway behind them.

At a table by the kitchen a bloke on his own with a phone and a computer open.

He belongs. He's the boss.

Frank figures they can't stay too long. It'd look suspicious.

As Frank and Jean approach the counter to pay, a woman comes down the stairway, walks through the kitchen and sits down with the boss.

Frank goes cold.

'Are you paying, Frank, or am I?'

Frank is frozen.

Jean can see that, behind the glasses and the outsize teeth, Frank's face has turned white.

'Frank?'

Frank takes out his card and pays.

Jean and Frank leave the Yum Yum and sit down again at the bus stop opposite.

Frank is shaking. Jean leans over and takes his hand.

They sit for about twenty minutes before Frank is able to talk.

'It was her, Jean. Sue May—the one who set me up. It was her that came down the stairway.'

'What are you going to do, Frank?'

Frank stares straight ahead. Then he turns to Jean. 'I don't know yet.'

Eventually he decides to get in his car and drive around to the back of the Yum Yum.

Jean says she'll keep an eye on the front door. If Sue May comes out, she'll text Frank. She promises to stay as long as Frank wants.

As dark is coming in, Sue May comes out the back and gets into a Merc. Pretty new.

Frank texts Jean to go home. Thanks her and says he'll be in touch.

Be careful, Frank, Jean texts back.

Frank follows Sue May in the Merc.

He is careful.

Sue May pulls into the driveway of a house in Strathfield. Not a dump. Worth a quid, that's for sure.

Frank stays watching for about four hours.

Nothing.

Sue May has to live there. She has obviously come up in the world. Her world. Her world of fucking people over.

What to do?

Frank is exhausted.

But something else is taking over. A calmness.

He drives back to Bondi. He goes for a swim. In the dark.

I know you're down there. The three of you, he thinks. All the swimmers at Bondi know. Three sharks live down below. Have done forever, they all reckoned.

You have to put it out of your mind. Just make sure you don't swim when the salmon are running. Could lose an arm or a leg. Arms and legs look like salmon to sharks.

Long deep strokes, a breath on every sixth stroke.

Frank is lying on his bed in his room at the Bondi Hotel.

After his thumping from the goons, Frank had moved. He'd packed a few clothes, his toothbrush and computer, and booked into the Bondi.

He parks his car a couple of streets back.

All-day parking. Not easy to find in Bondi. Not like when

he first moved here. When you could park on the footpath and nobody said anything.

And the Bondi has changed too.

One day, way back, when he'd first moved to the inner city, he came for a swim at Bondi. It had been hot but great.

The water. He couldn't describe the water. It made him joyous. Only way he could think of it. Different to the municipal pool where he trained.

He had been twenty-three.

Never forgot it. The beach was covered with beautiful girls. Tops off. He hadn't known where to look. So he'd gone across the road to the Bondi and sat upstairs in the open-air beer garden.

The pub had been sparkling white, with lots of character. Not like now—ordinary and five storeys. Frank had bought a beer. It was cold as, and it had a heavenly head on it.

Frank had felt great as he looked across at the beach and out into the ocean.

He'd reckoned that one day he was going to live by the beach.

That had been nearly fifty years ago.

And now this.

A fucked-up life.

Seeing Sue May has sent him into some sort of shock.

It was the same as in Hong Kong when the customs people opened up the soap and incense.

He knew immediately this was going to turn out bad. He knew no one would believe he was innocent.

His body had gone into meltdown. The nerves in his body had done things he couldn't believe. He'd pissed himself.

And now he'd seen the woman who did this to him.

They grab Bonnie from out front of the Icebergs.

Straight into the back of the car. One hand over her mouth, another on her throat.

She can't breathe. Is sure she's about to die. Suffocate.

Then they take their hands away.

Bonnie gulps in air. She tries to scream, but nothing comes out.

'Don't scream. Sit still and you will live.'

There is one driving and two in the back on either side of her.

They hold Bonnie and bind her wrists.

Clinton posts the letter at the post office.

He buys an envelope with a stamp attached, writes the numbers on the inside and sends it to Nula Ondine. He writes that Nula should please pass on the letter to the swimming man if anything bad happens to him. Tells her it's the lady's number.

Then he gets himself a pepper pie and a chocolate milk.

Good pies in Australia.

He walks back to his house and lies down on the old lounge the House of Friendship had found for him.

That Jean O'Connor is a very good lady. She's done heaps for the Sudanese community.

When the knock comes, Clinton gets up and opens the door.

It's the lady and she isn't alone.

Three men come in with her. Two hold him and the other belts his face and hits him in the stomach.

Clinton can't breathe.

'What did you tell the swimming man about me, Clinton?'

'Nothing. I told him nothing. Just like I tell you. That Michael made calls from the House of Friendship. That's all. That's true on my mother's life.'

The lady nods to the men.

Two pick him up and one opens the window.

Clinton lives on the third floor of the block of flats. He likes his home in Australia. The Australians have been good to him, not like back in Sudan where he was always running from the soldiers.

Being three floors up gives Clinton a view.

He thinks about how much he likes the view as he is thrown through the window and head first onto the concrete.

The window is closed and the lady leaves with the three men.

Professor Leong wants to know why Frank missed his last appointment, and why he hadn't rung to cancel.

'I couldn't make it. I was busy. And I didn't want to see you, anyway.'

'Why, Frank?'

'It gets in the way of my revenge.'

The professor looks at Frank. Then he gets up from his desk and walks to the little basin in the office. 'Water, Frank?'

Frank ignores the question. 'Is that good stuff, Professor? Good stuff to try to understand me, Professor?'

They sit looking at each other.

Frank leans over and pours himself a glass of water. 'I found her. Sue May.'

The professor nods and takes a sip from his glass. Then he puts the glass down on the desk. 'And so, Frank, what happens now?'

Frank leans forward. 'You tell me, Professor. You're the expert. You're working me out. Will I kill her, do you reckon?'

The professor looks at Frank intently.

'No, you won't kill her, Frank. You're not a killer. Go to the police. Tell them you've found Sue May.'

It's in the paper the next day. The death of Clinton Hanifa.

There's a photo of Clinton smashed on the cement. It isn't a pretty picture. His black head covered in blood.

The papers reckon it's drug related. Sudanese gangs taking over the drug scene. God, they talk shit.

But Frank knows it's because of him. Has to be.

Maybe he's getting close. Frank likes that thought. Fuels his revenge.

But he doesn't like that he got Clinton killed.

Frank sits in his car in the laneway behind the Yum Yum.

Not too close. Doesn't want to be noticed.

He's been there since ten. Listens to James Valentine at two. He loves James. James never talks down to his listeners. James's show reminds you how clever the average bloke or woman is. And funny.

Fuck, people are funny.

Frank likes it when people talk about the strange habits of their partners. How they only hang certain clothes on the line with certain colour pegs, and things like that.

It's seven o'clock when the van drives up and parks in the Yum Yum driveway.

Eight girls climbed out. Young. Seventeen, eighteen years.

Sue May comes out onto a balcony and stands at the top of the outside stairs, looking down.

Night duty.

Then another eight girls walk past her down the steps. They get into the van. Just one heavy escorting them along with the driver.

Asian. All of them.

Frank follows the van to a block of flats only a couple of k away. Still Campsie, he reckons. Two up, two down and only one front door entrance into the block.

The girls stream in and lights started flicking on in all the flats. The heavy follows them.

———

Bonnie has been sitting on a chair for hours.

She's tied to the chair. Arms and legs. Can't move.

There's a pillowcase over her head. She wants to scream.

Wants to scream for Frank. For Frank to get her.

But she knows it doesn't work like that. No one will come get her; they'll make sure of it.

She has shouted a few times, but nothing. So she gives up shouting and decides to wait.

You learn patience through swimming. Wait until the right moment to go for it. It will come. Don't waste energy.

She hears the door open.

Not sure how many are now in the room.

A few.

'Where is your father?'

Asian Australian voice. Female.

'How the fuck would I know?'

She is smacked across the face. It hurts.

'We know he is no longer at his home. So where is he?'

Bonnie can't help it. She starts to cry.

Hates herself for it.

———

Frank likes Jean's house.

It smelled of home.

His house used to smell like this when it was the three of them, him, Mary and Bonnie. Seems an age ago.

Epping is a leafy middle-class suburb about ten k to the north of the city. Not grand, but content. Sort of like Jean.

They have a cup of tea and some shortbread Jean has made.

'Frank, Nula Ondine gave me a letter for you. She said it was from Clinton.'

Frank nods and takes the letter.

'Clinton told her to give it to you if anything happened to him. Please, Frank, nothing must happen to bring shame on the House of Friendship. The House of Friendship provides so much for these people who have so little. I trust you, Frank, but I am worried.'

What a terrific woman Jean is. She could blast him. Tell him to fuck off out of her life.

But she doesn't.

'The government has withdrawn one hundred thousand dollars from our funding for the next two years. That's enough for us to cope with.'

Frank gets up and kisses Jean on the cheek. 'Believe me, I would never do anything to hurt you or the House of Friendship.'

Then he leaves.

The call comes in the middle of the night. Frank is in Hong Kong, running down an alleyway. A police siren is getting louder and louder as the police car gets closer and closer.

And then it isn't a police siren. It's his phone.

'We have your daughter, Mr Testy.'

And then a click. Nothing.

That was it. It was a silent number.

Frank is wide awake now.

Fuck.

Think.

Someone has Bonnie.

But they could be lying.

Fuck. Fuck. Fuck.

They wouldn't be lying. They want him and they intend to get him through Bonnie. So she must be alive.

Keep it together, Frank.

If emotion takes over, the part of the brain needed for good decisions closes down. And right now Frank needs to make good decisions.

Really good decisions.

Why does he feel so calm?

Frank picks up his phone. He scrolls to Bonnie's number.

Should he?

And then he does. He dials Bonnie.

It rings.

A man answers. 'It took you longer than we expected, Mr Testy.'

Frank says nothing.

'If you want to see your daughter again, you will do as I say.'

'I want my daughter. I want to speak to Bonnie.'

'You are not in charge of this conversation, Mr Testy, so please listen.'

Frank listens as he is told where he needs to go and at what time.

And then there is a moment of quiet before he hears her.

'Dad, I'm sorry.'

And that's it.

He knows Bonnie is alive.

He also knows where Bonnie is right now.

Botany. An industrial suburb on the south side of Sydney. Sitting on the bay where Captain James Cook landed in 1788.

Bonnie had told him after Mary died that, if he ever needed to find her, he should open the Find My app she had downloaded there for him.

It's still there.

She had forgotten to trash it after their falling-out.

Frank's car radio says it's 3.03 am.

His car is parked in Dent Street. Find My shows Bonnie to be by the corner of Dent and Wilson.

At the end of Wilson is a park that runs into Foreshore Road. And then there was the bay.

But which house is Bonnie in?

Most of the houses are dark. Three have lights on inside. Two in Dent and one in Wilson.

Frank gets out of his car.

But what now?

His heart is racing.

He has to calm down.

This isn't his game, going up against thugs. Doesn't know where to start.

But he does know about goals. And his goal is to find his daughter.

Take a breath.

And another.

Focus.

Frank goes to the boot. Opens it and takes out the jack.

Another breath.

Frank moves down Dent.

At the first house he slides beneath the front window and looks inside. The hall light gives a view into a lounge room.

Empty.

Frank moves down the side of the house. Very silent. No car in the driveway.

Frank waits and listens.

Still silent.

He moves back out to Dent Street.

At the next house there's a car in the driveway.

A Toyota.

How do the Japs do it? Bloody Toyotas everywhere. Every second car in Australia seems to be a Toyota. And what really shits you is they are good. No wonder Australia doesn't have a car industry. Bloody Japs are too good.

This one isn't so good, though.

Few dents on the right-hand side panel.

Dents on Dent Street.

Frank slips past the Toyota to a side window where there's a light. He looks through the window. Sees a woman sitting on the side of a bed holding a baby.

This isn't the house, that's for sure.

Now the only house with a light on is in Wilson Street.

Frank walks around the corner and stands in the shadows.

In the driveway is a large four-wheel drive. Brand spanking new. Black.

Frank looks at his watch.

3.45 am.

It will be light in two hours.

He crawls past the four-wheeler.

Down the drive.

Quietly.

He has no idea what to do if Bonnie is in there.

Take a breath.

Think.

He goes back to the four-wheeler. He bends down to the front left wheel. He uncovers the tyre valve and presses it. Air comes out.

Frank stays like that until the tyre is flat.

Then he moves back down the side of the house.

The instructions had been for him to meet them at 6 am in the car park of the Yarra Bay Sailing Club. That's about a ten-minute drive away.

Frank figures there will have to be movement soon. They have an appointment to keep.

With him.

And then the back door opens.

A thug emerges dragging Bonnie. She has a bag over her head. Her hands are tied in front of her.

They walk to the car. The thug opens the rear door.

Frank has instilled into his swimmers that you only get one chance.

Don't overthink things. Strike while the iron is hot.

So he does.

He smacks the thug across the side of the head with the jack. He puts all his strength into it.

The thug drops to the ground like a bag of wet cement.

Whole thing must have taken three seconds.

Frank grabs Bonnie.

'It's me, darling. Dad.'

He rips the bag off her head. She looks terrible.

'We need to run, Bon. Can you do that?'

She nods.

They take off.

Two more thugs come from the house. Frank hears a shout as they find their mate.

Frank and Bonnie race down Wilson, but not towards his car. Cars can be chased.

They head the other way. The Bay way.

Water.

The thugs jump in the car, turn it over and slam the accelerator.

But not so fast. A flat tyre.

Frank and Bonnie make it through the park, cross Fore-shore Road and stop.

The bay is in front of them. Out in the water are a few boats on buoys.

Frank takes Bonnie's wrists. Tries to break the ties. Plastic.

'We're going in. You have to trust me, Bon.'

She is in shock. Just looks at him.

He moves with her into the water.

Waist-high.

Then neck-high.

Then he's on his back. Hand under her chin. Striking out into the bay.

Looking back, he can make out the two thugs in the park, scanning the shore.

The streetlights don't help them much.

Frank and Bon haven't been seen.

———

This wasn't going to go down well with the lady. And it didn't.

The thug with the smashed head is no good to her, she tells them. Dump him.

And they do. Into the bay.

'Now find them both, please.'

Frank swims Bonnie out to one of the boats. One with an outboard motor.

Frank holds on to the boat with one hand. His legs are under his daughter's bum to keep her from sinking.

He places Bonnie's wrists on either side of a propeller blade and carefully moves her hands backwards and forwards across it.

Finally the plastic gives way.

They stay by the boat for another ten minutes.

'Can you swim, Bon?'

'Yes,' she says.

And they begin their swim.

Frank tells her how much she means to him.

Tells her about the funny things that happened with her when she was little.

Tells her how much he misses Mary.

Tells her he was an idiot.

Asks for forgiveness.

And then Bonnie reaches up and touches his face.

And then they both cry.

———

Sue May goes to the safe behind the reception upstairs at the Yum Yum Massage Parlour. It was Friday lunchtime. She opens it and takes out the week's takings.

The girls are good. Know what's expected of them. To turn over the clients.

The more clients they turn over, the sooner they'll pay off their loan and get their passports back.

Stupid children. That will take years, and by then they'll have no value to the clients. No man will want them. No want, no money.

The takings were good. Over forty thousand dollars a day. A lot of it in cash. Tax man doesn't need to know about all the cash.

She puts the cash in a Coles supermarket bag and goes to the bank, same as every Friday.

Except this Friday Frank is watching.

She deposits just enough then the rest of the cash goes home in the Coles bag with Sue May, usually with a few groceries. She knew that was safest.

Who would guess what else was in the bag?

The Saturday morning papers have the story of the body found in Botany Bay.

Been dead a couple of days, the cops said. 'Unidentified at this stage.' Damage to the head meant 'suspicious circumstances'.

It isn't suspicious to Frank.

It was survival. Nothing suspicious about needing to survive.

———

Frank had taken Bonnie back to the Bondi Hotel. Put her into his bed. Sat with her through the day.

She woke a couple of times. Went back to sleep. Yelled a couple of times while sleeping. Frank held her hand.

Must have slept sixteen hours. Looked better for it.

They speak when she is strong enough. Gets some soup into her.

Frank offers to get her a room of her own, but Bonnie says no, she wants to stay with him. 'Is that alright?'

Of course it's alright.

Frank tells Bonnie he doesn't have a clue what they should do next. He has no doubt the thugs will be looking for them. That they are on someone's kill list.

Bonnie smiles and says Mary will look after them.

Frank can't believe he's such a softie.

Tears fill his eyes.

They spend the weekend inside the Bondi, resting and eating. Getting Bonnie's strength back.

She's a tough little thing, and come Monday she surprises Frank by suggesting a swim.

So they go for a swim together, something they haven't done for a very long time.

Frank lets Bonnie lead. Just kicks in behind her.

Long deep strokes, a breath on every sixth stroke.

On the way back, from north to south, Frank moves to Bonnie's side.

They match it stroke for stroke.

Frank can't help smiling.

Smiling while swimming. A new one.

They reach the north end. Swim into the beach.

'How was that?'

Bonnie is beaming. 'Loved it,' she says. 'Missed it.'

As they dry off, Frank looks up at the balcony of the Icebergs.

It's been four weeks since he'd started his search for the cunt who ruined his life. But here he is now, with his daughter, having finished a swim. He's glad he isn't dead.

Is this where it should end? Should he and Bonnie leave his revenge behind and start again in another state?

Others have done it.

New place. New name. New life.

But he knows they wouldn't allow that.

Back at the Bondi, Frank looks at the letter from Nula Ondine.

Clinton's letter, with a phone number scribbled on the inside and the words 'The Lady' alongside the number.

Nothing else. Just that. A number and a name. If you could call it a name.

What does he have to lose?

He keys in the number.

A name came up on the screen.

Frank stares at his phone. He doesn't connect the call.

Bonnie goes in first. The Yum Yum Korean Restaurant is about three-quarters full.

She sits opposite the counter at the front and orders japchae. Always loved noodles. Mary had introduced her to Asian food from an early age.

Bonnie feels so blessed to have had Mary for a mum. God, you can get lucky.

Frank comes in and goes to the back of the restaurant. The boss is sitting opposite at his computer.

Frank has his silly teeth in and is wearing the glasses and beanie. He orders bulgogi. Doesn't know the first thing about Korean food, but marinated beef barbecue sounds okay.

Frank opens the newspaper he's brought with him and begins to read, keeping an eye on the boss and the back stairs. In his pocket he has plastic ties, masking tape and a switchblade knife.

Sue May would be leaving for the bank in about half an hour.

The japchae and the bulgogi come at the same time.

Frank vacuums up the bulgogi and asks for the bill. Pays cash. Stays reading the paper, in no hurry to leave.

Bonnie gets up and goes to the counter.

'I'm not paying for that shit,' she says to the woman at the counter. She has eaten about half the japchae.

The lady at the counter says she has to pay.

Bonnie starts yelling. The Yum Yum is a dump. She has no intention of paying.

There's a shouting match.

Suddenly the boss gets up. 'You go. You go.' He grabs Bonnie by the shoulder and pushes her out the front door and onto the footpath. 'You never come back,' he shouts.

Bonnie storms off down the street.

The boss walks back inside. He apologises to the customers: 'Stupid woman. She not come back. Sorry.' He goes back to his computer.

The table opposite is empty now.

Frank's newspaper sits on the Formica table.

As soon as the boss had pushed Bonnie out the front door, Frank hurried to the stairs leading up to the massage parlour and Sue May.

Now, he climbs the stairs quickly and quietly.

He is shit-scared.

Calm it, Frank.

Deep breaths.

Control.

Focus.

There is a door at the top of the stairs.

He could still back out.

But, as he told his swimmers, you can't live your life in fear and avoidance.

Frank carefully opens the door.

Sue May has her back to him. A Coles bag is on the counter by the till.

'This knife will go straight through your neck if you move or say a word.'

Sue May freezes.

Frank orders her to put her hands behind her back.

She does as he asks. He clips two plastic ties around her wrists.

With the knife still at her throat, Frank takes the Coles bag and looks inside. There's a lot of dough in there. A week's worth of fucking money.

Frank smiles at his little joke. *Fucking money.*

Focus, you idiot.

Frank covers Sue May's mouth with masking tape and pushes her ahead of him down the corridor. He opens a door marked *Private*. There is a bed and a sofa, and a desk with a phone on it.

He shoves Sue May down on the bed and puts plastic ties around her ankles. Then he takes off his beanie and glasses and removes the funny teeth.

'Remember me, Sue May?'

She stares at Frank. He doesn't know if she recognises him or not.

'You fucked up my life, Sue May, and now I'm fucking yours.'

He picks up the phone and dials 000. When the call is answered, he asks for the cops. Says he wants to report a robbery that is in motion at the Yum Yum Massage Parlour above the Yum Yum Barbecue Restaurant in Campsie. Says if they hurry they'll find a whole lot of Asian women working as prostitutes. Reckons they might be sex slaves.

Then he hangs up.

Closes the door marked *Private*.

Goes down the stairs to the street with the Coles bag in his hand.

Back at the Bondi, Frank and Bonnie count the money. One hundred and fifteen grand.

Fuck, that's a lot of moolah.

They start laughing. Can't stop. Adrenaline and relief.

Wow. What have they pulled off? Are they crims stealing from crims?

Probably.

Frank hasn't been on such a high since his swimmers won gold at the Olympics.

But he knows it isn't over yet. He knows Sue May will be on the phone quick smart. And he knows they'll be looking for him. Real hard.

Sue May isn't the end of the line. Frank understands that. His revenge has a way to go.

A little way yet.

Saturday night is going to be a big night at the Icebergs.

Big fundraiser. Frank is taking Bonnie. He is also taking Jean.

The Icebergs is jumping when the three of them arrive.

The committee is crowded around the bar, laughing heartily at some stupid story Bill is telling.

Such a fuckwit. Never knows when to shut up.

Frank and Bonnie and Jean grab drinks and head out onto the balcony.

It's a warm night. The ocean is calm. The moon full.

As the evening drifts on, the balcony fills. Too nice not to be out here.

Bill Gower and his wife join Frank. Bill tells Frank he understands the last months must have been difficult. Hopes he might consider joining the committee.

Frank is stunned. This is the first time his situation has been acknowledged.

Frank introduces Bonnie and Jean. Tells Bill and his wife about Jean's work at the House of Friendship.

While they chat, Frank notices Tony McGee and Lee arrive.

Tony sees Frank and waves. He and Lee make their way over.

As Bill and his missus head inside to kick off proceedings, Bill asks Frank to join him fishing the next morning. 'The salmon are running. Six o'clock at Rose Bay wharf, Frank. See you there.'

Frank watches Bill handling the emceeing as though born to it. The money starts pouring in.

On the balcony, Tony wants to know how Frank's investigation has been going.

'Gave it up, Tony. Realised I was behaving like an idiot. What could I find out? I'm a swimming coach, not a cop.'

Lee is interested to know how Frank and Jean came to know each other. Jean tells Lee that the House of Friendship is always looking for supporters. People who have some ability to help the refugees and migrants and their children.

Frank has been great at teaching them to swim. Not a lot of migrants can swim. 'I wouldn't want them to come swimming at Bondi without some knowledge of the ocean. Too dangerous, Lee.'

Bonnie begins to cough. 'I'm not feeling too good,' she says. 'Can you help me to the toilet, please?'

Jean and Lee gently steer Bonnie through the crowd to the ladies.

Frank and Tony stand looking out to the ocean. 'Tony, I need to talk to you. Can we go outside for a sec? It's pretty important.'

Frank and Tony leave the Icebergs and walk towards Campbell Parade.

At the stairs to the beach Tony stops and asks Frank what it is he wants to discuss.

Frank says, 'No, down on the beach, Tony. It's more private. It'll only take a minute, I promise.'

Tony says it had better be good. The girls will wonder where they are.

On the beach Frank stops. Tells Tony if it wasn't for him he wouldn't have been able to work out what happened to him in Hong Kong. But, thanks to Tony, he's pretty sure he knows who's behind it.

Frank pulls out his phone.

Dials.

'This is the person who is dealing in the drugs, Tony.'

He hands his phone to Tony.

After a few rings, the phone is answered.

'Hello, Frank.'

'Go on, talk to her, Tony. It's Lee.'

Tony ends the call. Stands looking at Frank.

Frank puts his arm around his shoulder. 'Are we mates, Tony?'

Tony doesn't answer.

'You're a cunt, Tony.'

Frank opens the switchblade and holds it against Tony's neck. 'Tell you what we are going to do, mate. We are going for a little swim. You and me, Tony.'

'Don't be an idiot, Frank. I know nothing about any drugs. Neither does Lee.'

'Tony, I was given a number for the lady behind the killing of Clinton Hanifa. And guess what? It was already on my phone. Now, get your pants off. Shoes and socks and don't be a fuckwit.

'But if you choose to be a fuckwit, then I will shove this blade straight into your neck.

'Are you faster than me, Tony?

'Maybe.

'But I trained swimmers, Tony.

'Trained them to be fast off the mark.

'Are you faster off the mark than me, Tony?

'Do you really want to find out, mate?'

Tony slowly strips down to his undies.

'Now your shirt.'

He does as he's told.

'Put your hands out front.'

Franks pulls a plastic tie tight on Tony's wrists. He tells Tony to lie down on his stomach. Frank then strips down to his speedos.

'Okay, Frank,' says Tony. 'Let's talk. How much do you want?'

Frank doesn't answer. He lifts Tony up and pushes him into the surf.

'Frank, we don't need to do this,' says Tony. 'We're mates. I gave you the list of passengers.'

'Yeah, I thought about that. But you knew me, Tony. You knew I'd find a way if you didn't give them to me.

This way you could keep an eye on me. Watch what I was up to.'

Frank grabs Tony around the chest and strikes out through the surf.

'Don't try anything. I have the knife in my Speedos.'

———

In the ladies' toilet, Bonnie and Jean stand in front of Lee, who is against the wall. They have instructions from Frank to keep Lee in the toilet for twenty minutes after the call.

'Don't test us, Lee. Just don't test us,' Jean warns.

———

The swell isn't big and Frank drags Tony out past the last break. Then he continues to strike out further into the ocean.

'Are you scared, Tony?'

Tony doesn't answer.

'Your mind is in panic mode. I know that feeling. I have to convince my swimmers to ignore the panic. Concentrate. Put all their training into each swim.

'But it isn't easy. Takes practice. And their lives aren't at stake. Just their careers.

'Your life is at stake, Tony. My fuckin word it is.'

When Frank looks back at Bondi it's all lights. Campbell Parade is happy.

Tony is not happy. 'What the fuckin hell do you think you're doing, Frank?'

'Taking my revenge, Tony.'

Tony begins to whimper. 'I'm loaded, Frank. You can have anything you want. Please. Take me back.'

Frank figures they're about two kilometres out by now. He stops swimming and treads water.

'Okay, Tony. This will do. You know the salmon are running, don't you? And our three mates are down below. They don't usually give a fuck about us, but I'll bet they're salivating over the salmon now.

'I would love to let you go right here, Tony. Wouldn't take long for you to sink with your wrists tied. Maybe that's what I should do?'

'Please, Frank. I'm begging you.'

Frank thinks for a moment. He knows he's not a killer. But he has changed. He is a new Frank Testy.

'You explain to me how this all started, Tony, and I'll cut you loose.'

Frank can feel Tony's body relax.

'I met Lee ten years back in a hotel in Hong Kong while I was there on a layover. I'd see her every time I flew in.

'Then I started bringing some drugs back into Sydney with me. It was easy.

'After a while Lee came to live with me in Sydney. She had people here involved in all sorts of stuff.

'I retired from flying. Didn't need it. We had it all working nicely.'

Frank reaches down into his Speedos.

'Fuck, Tony, the knife's fallen out. You're on your own.'

He lets Tony go.

Tony splashes around. Takes in water. 'No, Frank—please.'

Frank grabs him.

'Just joking.'

He cuts the plastic tie and moves away from Tony.

'There's Bondi, Tony. Couple of ks away. Think you can make it?'

Tony treads water. Stares at Bondi in the distance.

'Frank, I can't make it on my own. It's years since I swam at the Icebergs. You've got to help me.'

Frank moves away a bit, stops and yells back, 'You're a cunt, Tony.'

Then he resumes swimming.

Long deep strokes, with a breath on every sixth stroke.

At six o'clock the next morning, Frank boards Bill's boat in Rose Bay for a day's salmon fishing.

By eight o'clock they are off Bondi, about a kilometre and a half from the beach.

The salmon are sure running. It's good fishing.

'Bit of a commotion on the beach, Frank,' says Bill.

And there is.

Looks like cops.

Bonnie wakes in the Bondi Hotel.

Goes downstairs for coffee on the Parade.

There's a fair bit of commotion happening down on the beach.

Cops and onlookers.

A body has been found.

———

Lee sits waiting for the evening plane to Hong Kong. She watches the news on the television in the lounge.

A body has washed ashore at Bondi.

An arm and a leg are missing.

The person's clothes have been found on the beach.

People should realise how dangerous it is to swim at night.

Lee's flight is called.

She gets up and heads for her gate.

———

On Monday morning Jean finds a Coles bag with one hundred thousand dollars inside sitting on her desk at the House of Friendship.

———

'I let him go.'

Professor Leong looks at Frank.

Frank looks back at the professor.

'And now I'm letting you go, Professor.'

———

Frank sits on the verandah of the Icebergs.

It's a beautiful hot summer's day.

A light westerly is blowing.

The surf is about four feet.

The surfers are happy.

The bathers are happy.

A large glass of beer is sitting in front of Frank.

Frank picks it up and drinks.

He puts the glass down and wipes the foam from his mouth.

'Hi, Dad.'

'Hi, Bon.'

Bonnie sits opposite Frank and looks to the waves.

Frank smiles.

He is happy.

NIGHTMARE

We landed at John F. Kennedy airport ten minutes early, at 8.50 pm. It was Sunday night, the same day we'd left Sydney. Going home we would lose a day. Molly and I had argued about going Qantas or United. United won because of its better frequent flyer program.

'People don't get killed flying Qantas,' I said.

This was Molly's first trip to the States. I had been to San Francisco in my last year of high school. I went for a junior rugby international. I didn't remember much, but I knew I'd liked it. That was twenty-eight years ago and for two weeks.

The ride from the airport to the Gramercy Park Hotel seemed to take ages. On part of the ride it was like driving through a town that had been evacuated—the buildings weren't falling down but there was no one about. The cab driver was Iranian; it said so on the ID displayed on the dashboard. What must it have been like for him during the hostage crisis? It wouldn't be nice being hated by two hundred and fifty million people.

The Gramercy Park Hotel was downtown, alongside Gramercy Park on Twenty-first Street. It was an old hotel in need of a coat of paint, but it had plenty of character, with a large piano bar just off the entrance. Our room was decent and looked out over the park. Molly handed the porter five dollars and asked him how close we were to Little Italy.

Although it was midnight we were both wide awake, it being only 2 pm Sydney time, so rather than argue for a good night's sleep and an early start the next day, I went along with Molly's enthusiasm. The restaurant was packed and noisy, the meal was delicious and, apart from Molly's stupid flirtation with the waiter (he looked like John Travolta), we had a good time.

'You have a beautiful wife,' the maître d' told me on the way out. 'You are a lucky man.'

'Thanks,' I said.

A cab was just dropping someone off out the front of the restaurant so we grabbed it.

Molly and I had been married seventeen years. We met when I was twenty-five and just about to open a dental practice. We were seated at the same table at a ball in the Menzies Hotel in Sydney and she belonged to another bloke. I stared at her the whole evening, and then asked for her number while he was off having a pee. She wouldn't give it to me. She wasn't rude or anything; she just said, 'I'm with

someone else tonight and I don't think it's right, do you?'
I sort of agreed, but I kept staring.

Three weeks later she called me at the surgery.

'Do you still want my number?' she said.

Six months later we were married.

In the taxi we sat in silence, each staring out at the streets
of this huge city. The last couple of years of our marriage
hadn't been real great. Not terrible, but not real great. We
were obviously moving into a new phase of life. The children
didn't need us so much now; they had their own friends
and, in fact, we hardly saw them, what with studying and
sport and general socialising. In another couple of years Phil
would be at university and Richard would follow him a year
later. I suspected that I might be going through a mid-life
crisis. I seemed to be treading water. My practice was very
successful, but did I want to be looking into mouths for the
next twenty years?

I needed a change, but what? The economy was terrible;
a change seemed out of the question. And then, two years
ago, Molly had started working again for a publisher. She
was doing well, but I resented her attention being taken
away from me and the family. We'd had more rows during
the past two years than in the whole of the previous fifteen
years put together. I hoped this holiday would bring us
closer again.

'Look at the steam pouring out of the manholes,' Molly
said. 'It's sort of eerie, isn't it?'

'I suppose so,' I said.

'I feel like I'm in a movie.' She laughed. 'I'm in *The Godfather*.'

'One, Two or Three?' I asked.

'Oh, I don't know—all of them I guess.'

As we pulled up to the hotel, the meter showed six dollars, fifty cents. I put seven one-dollar bills into the tray cut into the Perspex shield. We got out and headed for the hotel entrance.

'Hey, fella,' shouted the taxi driver, holding the seven dollars in his fist.

I hurried back. 'I'm sorry—haven't I given you enough?'

But he cut me off. 'I don't think you meant to give me this.' He was holding up a hundred-dollar bill.

'Jesus, thanks, mate.'

I exchanged the hundred for a ten.

'Thanks again,' I said as he pulled out and drove off into the night. Don't knock New York cabbies to me, I thought as I walked into the hotel. Bet that wouldn't have happened at home.

It was 4.06 am when I woke, according to the clock radio by the bed. Molly was still asleep. I got up and walked to the window. Already there was someone jogging. An old man was wandering down the street on the far side of the park. Taxis kept gliding by. The night was alive. I was fascinated.

The old man would be curled up asleep in bed in a few minutes, I thought, as he climbed the stairs to the doorway of his apartment building. I watched him as he tried to open the door. He was having trouble. It wouldn't open. He turned and went back down the stairs.

What would he do now? I wondered.

He began climbing the stairs of the apartment building next door and he tried that door. No go. Then it struck me: he didn't live in either apartment. Down the steps he went. Would he try the next apartment? Yes. And the one after that? I wanted to wake Molly to share this strange piece of behaviour. Was he a thief, a serial killer, or just an old man looking for somewhere warm to doss? He tried his fifth door. It opened. In he went.

What now? I must have watched for ten minutes. He never came out. I went back to bed. When Molly woke me it was 11 am.

The next two days were spent discovering New York. The funny thing about New York is that so much of it is so familiar. Film and television have made us all New Yorkers. We know Central Park and Times Square and often a street or shopfront brings on a sense of déjà vu. It is as noisy, loud and rude as you'd expect, but the energy of the place is what excites you. You feel you mustn't stop. The other thing I felt was the exhaustion that came from having to be on my guard the whole time. Look like tourists and we'll be mugged—keep moving, I kept reminding myself.

But nothing happened. We shopped until we dropped, and took ourselves off to lunch and dinner at great little places that Molly had sussed out from the concierge.

Our plan was to have a week in New York and about ten days in California, which included a drive from Los Angeles to San Francisco, spending time in the wine region.

Our only contact in New York was Anthony Couples, one of the VPs at Penguin Books, the publishing company Molly worked for in Australia. Anthony had invited us to have dinner with him and his wife on the Wednesday night at an Upper East Side restaurant called Palma. Because of Wednesday night, I think I became his best friend forever.

The restaurant was full. We arrived first and had a drink at the bar. The crowd was a money crowd, you could smell it. Successful people, confident, at ease, and aware of everyone who entered. No one knew us of course, but Molly certainly attracted some attention. And why not? She looked extremely beautiful tonight; a bloke would have to be a fool not to have noticed her.

Anthony Couples was warm and welcoming. He gave Molly a big hug, shook my hand and introduced his wife, Laura. She was obviously from somewhere in South America, though I never did get around to asking where. Anthony was obviously known here, and we were graciously shown to our table.

I must say, I was in a very good mood. Getting away from work and my worries, together with the fun of the last few days and two quick beers, had me pretty loose. And the Couples were great: easy to talk to, interested and funny. We laughed a lot and my story about the hundred-dollar bill and the cabbie was a new one on them. Molly and Anthony talked quite a bit about the publishing scene and Laura filled me in on a business administration course she was doing.

The table next to us was what you'd call a yuppie foursome. As I listened to Laura, I began to pick up that I was the butt of a few of their jokes. Things like 'obviously a farmer' and 'convict clothing' floated across from their table. Anthony became aware of it and I could see that he was embarrassed. He touched Molly on the hand mid-speech and said, 'I'm sorry, but I'm sure that type exists everywhere.'

I told him not to worry, caught the waiter's eye and, in my best Australian, ordered another bottle of red. I got up to go to the toilet and as I passed the foursome I could hear a take-off of 'Another bottle of red, thanks, mate'. They all laughed.

On my return, the waiter was delivering their dinner. I couldn't help myself: a slight stumble, a hand to the back of the waiter and four pastas found their way very nicely into the chests and laps of the two men, and unfortunately onto the face of one of the women. Apologising profusely, I blamed my awkwardness on my 'farmer's thighs', and offered to pay for everyone's meals.

We ended up back at Anthony and Laura's apartment for drinks. Anthony had not stopped laughing since the mishap. At one stage Laura thought he'd have a heart attack.

'I love you, I love you, I love you,' he kept saying to me.

Eventually he quietened down and over the next hour they persuaded us to change our plans and fly to Las Vegas at the end of the week, meet them there for the weekend and drive from Las Vegas to LA.

We flew into Vegas late Friday night and checked into the Flamingo. Anthony had explained that, although it was the first casino built and there were many more modern hotels, the Flamingo had the best food, some character and you get a good room for a fraction of the cost of the more upmarket places. We were to meet the Couples there on Saturday morning.

Molly was awake when the phone rang.

'Hi,' she said. 'Oh no, what bad luck! No, no, don't be silly, we'll be alright.'

She had my attention as she hung up.

'Anthony and Laura have to go to Chicago. Business. So I guess it's just us, darling,' she said as she bent down to give me a kiss.

The two of us had had a terrific week. No quarrels, no pressures. No insecurity. That had been a part of my problem recently. I knew it. I'd suspected for a while that Molly wished she was with someone else. Not that I thought she was having an affair, but I felt that I wasn't good enough for her. The way she'd respond to other men at times made me think she resented being married to me.

Of course I'd talk myself out of thinking like this, but then the doubts would creep back in. After all, I was just a bloody dentist. How boring could you get?

But this week she'd been warm and affectionate, and that made me respond to her in a much more personable way. It was possible she was still in love with me, I thought. I knew I was in love with her.

Vegas is a hole. It's tacky, cheap and nasty. It's also popular. Americans have been coming to Vegas for decades to see Perry Como or Frank Sinatra. Barbra Streisand plays Vegas. I'm sure Bruce Springsteen will get there one day.

Gambling made Vegas, and is still its core business. As soon as you get out of the plane you're confronted by slot machines. There is no airport in the world like Vegas. Huge video screens compete to show you what's on where. Showgirls and magicians and illusionists decked out in gear that Elvis Presley would have been embarrassed to wear jump out at you.

Saturday and Sunday were spent by the pool. Sure, we looked around and caught a show Saturday night, but Vegas is in the desert and the days are hot so we took it easy. That part was good after the hustle and bustle of New York. We both had tans by Sunday evening.

We'd fixed up a rental car for the morning, intending to check out about ten. That night, there was an Ice Capades show on at the Flamingo; it was sure to capture the spirit of Vegas, so a silly night was assured. Dinner and the show were at nine. A drink at the bar beforehand would help us through it.

We got talking to a bloke from Florida who'd spent a bit of time in Australia. He designed golf courses.

'Do people from Florida do anything but play golf?' Molly asked.

Our new friend laughed. 'Yeah, tennis is big,' he said.

His name was Joe. There are probably a lot of Joes in Vegas. Anyway, Joe joined us for dinner; he was good company. Just as well, because the show stunk. When the waiter presented the bill, Joe offered to pay.

'No way,' I said, 'our treat.' I handed my Visa card to the waiter. We still had beers to finish. Joe excused himself for the men's room.

'Don't drink mine while I'm away,' he said, winking at Molly.

Fifteen minutes passed. Joe was obviously doing more than a pee.

I called the waiter over and asked for my receipt and card.

'But I gave it to your friend after he signed it.'

'It wasn't his card,' I said. 'Didn't you check the signature?'

'I'm sorry, sir, I knew he was at this table. Where is he now?'

That was a good question. Molly looked at me. 'We've just been ripped off,' she said.

Back in the room I cancelled the card. Luckily the hotel had taken a copy when we checked in, so I told the Visa people to honour that bill.

'Angry?' Molly asked.

'Seething,' I answered. 'How could I be such a fool? Makes me want to fly home tomorrow.'

Molly wouldn't have any of that, of course. She still had her credit card, the car was paid for and in two days we'd be in LA, where I'd pick up my brand-new Visa card.

'You look good when you're annoyed,' she said.

'Do I?'

She put her arms around me. 'Let's go to bed.'

We did and I stopped being annoyed.

We had two choices: the Interstate 15 would take us directly to San Bernardino then on to the I-10 and into LA, a drive of five or six hours straight through. Instead, we chose to head south, skirting the Arizona border before heading west into Palm Springs. This meant we could have an overnight stop and enjoy the desert.

It was almost midday by the time we got away, and within an hour the peace and quiet and stark beauty of the desert made me forget about Joe and the circus called Vegas.

I had a fifty-dollar bill in my wallet. Most of that went on tips and sandwiches to munch during the drive ahead.

We decided to make a picnic of it and took a side road to the Colorado River. We had a swim and let the sun dry us off.

'Hungry?' asked Molly. She stood in a dainty white bra and panties, squeezing her hair.

'Sure am,' I said. 'Sure am.'

She smiled. 'Get the sandwiches.'

The sun makes you feel good. It enriches you. I felt like a battery on charge. How long was it since we'd done this? Never, really! Most holidays were with the kids or with friends, and everything was pre-planned.

I looked at Molly. Her eyes were closed. Was she asleep, or just miles away?

'You're still in good nick for a man your age, darling.'

'I'm only forty-two,' I snapped.

'I know, darling, and you're in very good shape for forty-two.'

Her eyes remained closed. I smiled. At least she was thinking of me.

We got back on the I-95 and headed down through Needles, intending to join the I-10 at a place called Blythe, but Molly sighted a turn-off at the Colorado River Aqueduct that would shorten our journey time to Palm Springs.

The road wasn't the best and evening was coming on fast. About twenty miles in, we hit Rice. If we'd blinked, we'd have missed it. Rice consists of one building: a sort of bar with about six booths and a fifties-type motel attached.

The motel must have had about eight rooms. I wondered how often they were used.

I intended driving through, but Molly suddenly sprang to life.

'Let's stay here. Look, we can even eat and get a room. Much better than Palm Springs. No one I know has ever stayed in Rice.'

The bloke behind the bar was fat. And I mean fat! We approached and exchanged pleasantries, if grunts pass for pleasantries.

'We'd like a room and a couple of steaks later on,' I said.

'Plastic,' he replied.

I turned to Molly and she gave me her Visa from her purse. The barman grabbed the card, looked at it then handed it back.

'This is out of date as of yesterday.'

I stared at him. What was this bullshit? Who was doing this to me?

'He's right,' said Molly, checking the card.

'Take traveller's cheques?' I asked.

'American Express?' he asked.

'What else?' I replied and undid my right shoe.

Molly gave me a what-are-you-doing? look.

I removed my shoe and took out ten fifty-dollar American Express traveller's cheques.

'You can't be too careful,' I said as I passed him four of the bills. He looked at them, one after the other.

'Sure can't,' he said. 'These are no good. Can't read the serial numbers.'

I grabbed them from him. I looked at them and then at the other six. The movement of my feet had left me with ten blue pieces of paper worth zilch.

'Fuck, fuck, fuck, fuck!'

We went back outside and stood by the car. I knew we were in a fix, but how bad a fix? I took a deep breath. 'Alright,' I said. 'We've got enough petrol to get us to Palm Springs, but then what?'

Molly shrugged. 'No use ringing Anthony for advice; he's in Chicago and I don't have his number. I could ring his office—they'd know where he was.'

'Sure,' I said, 'and what'll you say? We've lost one credit card, the other's expired and my husband's foot ruined our traveller's cheques.'

A car behind us beeped. What now?

'Can I help?'

He was in his early thirties, behind the wheel of a not-so-old station wagon. I'd noticed him in one of the booths in the bar.

'Heard what happened in there.'

We walked over to the car.

He had a nice smile. 'Need a bed for the night, right?'

'More importantly, I need petrol,' I said.

'No problem. Two forty-four-gallon drums of it on the property. Wife's always running out.'

He thrust his hand out the window: 'Jerry Sermac.'

I shook it. 'David Brody, and this is my wife, Molly.'

'Follow me,' he said. 'I live just down the road a bit.'

I turned to Molly.

'Let's go', she said.

As we got into the car, something nagged at me. Something was wrong, but I couldn't work out what. Later it dawned on me: Jerry Sermac hadn't paid any attention to Molly.

'Down the road a bit' turned out to be a forty-minute drive on a track as rough as guts. We passed an old, faded sign: DAUBY LAKE, it struggled to say. Then we were on it. A broken-down gate was pulled aside and two well-muscled dogs bounded down to us.

Jerry got out of his station wagon.

'Inside!' he shouted. 'Inside! Their bark's worse than their bite.'

We got out of our car.

'Doesn't look like much, but it's home. Come on inside.'

We followed him to the door of a fairly dilapidated jerry-built shack. I looked about. One night here will do us, I thought. I looked at Molly; she seemed to be enjoying herself.

'Honey, I'm home,' Jerry said. 'And guess what I've got with me?'

We walked into the room. I knew then we'd made a terrible mistake. On an old lounge chair sat a black-haired girl with eyes that stared straight through us. Next to her was a tall skinny bloke covered in tattoos. He was passing the girl a cigarette. He just grinned at us.

I grabbed Molly and turned for the door. As I did, from the corner of my eye I saw a fist coming straight for me. Someone had come in the door behind us. I hit the floor and scrambled to get up. Something slammed against my head as a boot hit my stomach. I screamed.

The struggle back to consciousness seemed to take forever.

Molly and I were alone. There was something misshapen about the room we were in. It was inside out. My frustration with this was enormous.

Of course, I was in a dream. I would keep moving to Molly and try to say the words 'I love you' but when I reached her, nothing would come out. Eventually she walked away from me.

I must have been out to it for about twenty minutes. As my head cleared, I found I really was in a room, but not the one Molly and I had entered. This was a bedroom, small and basic: unmade double bed, chest of drawers and wardrobe. Dirty orange curtains covered the one window. The stale smell of cigarettes filled the room. I was on my own and lying on the floor by the bed. My arms were tied behind my back and I wanted to throw up. I worked myself into a sitting position and turned towards the doorway.

'Pretty wife, pretty wife.'

It was the man on the lounge.

'Where is she?' I demanded. 'Where's Molly?'

And then I threw up.

The man laughed. 'Must have been something you ate.'

I tried to think. I looked up into the face of this man. Was he a man? How could he be? No man I knew or had known was capable of slamming such terror into my brain.

'Is my wife alright?'

I was surprised by the calmness of my voice. Why wasn't I shouting, screaming?

'Do you think I would harm such a beautiful woman? Come see for yourself.'

He grabbed me by the hair and dragged me through the door.

Molly was now sitting on the lounge beside the black-haired girl. Standing by her was a third man—the bastard who'd hit me, obviously. Our luggage was in the middle of the room, opened. Clothes were strewn everywhere.

Jerry Sermac, if that was his real name, was trying on one of my shirts. He bent down and picked up a pair of Molly's white panties. He smiled as he threw them across the room.

'These'll look good on you, Lila. Might turn me on some more.'

The black-haired girl picked them up.

I looked to Molly. 'You okay?'

She smiled and nodded. My brain raced. I was about to propose some stupid deal when Jerry grabbed my arms and pushed me towards a door leading to the kitchen.

'Promised you a bed for the night, didn't I? Let's go.'

He led me through the kitchen, out a back door and into a yard. The two dogs were chained to a steel spike that was driven into the ground. A large wooden crate was their home. About thirty feet beyond them was another stake and chain, alongside a piece of old foam rubber.

'Enjoy your stay.'

And I was pushed to the ground. A leg iron connected to the chain was snapped around my ankle.

As Jerry moved off, I called to him: 'Wait, Jerry—please wait.'

He turned to me.

'I don't understand what's going on,' I said. 'I really don't. How far do you intend to go with this?'

Jerry just smiled.

'I'm scared for my wife, Jerry, do you understand that? Please don't harm her. *Please.*'

He kept smiling. 'Sleep tight,' he said and went back to the house.

Darkness came in fast. I strained to hear.

The sounds of talking came from the house, but I couldn't make out any words. Music started. There was laughter. Through the window I could see people moving. Then I saw Molly. She was dancing. I couldn't see who with.

Then the tattooed man put his arm around her and began dancing close to her. They moved away from the window. I had to think positive. At least she could stand, move. She wasn't crying, so maybe they hadn't hurt her. But what would happen?

My head felt like it was about to explode. I started to crawl toward the house. As I did, the dogs sprang towards me. Their teeth looked like they could rip me to pieces. Fortunately, their chain forced them to stop a couple of metres from me.

I crawled back to my piece of foam rubber. Eventually the dogs withdrew to the crate. I was going to die in this place, I knew it.

The voices and laughter got louder. They were drinking. I couldn't hear Molly's voice, though. Then all went quiet. It must have been around midnight, I reckoned. I had no watch; that must have been taken while I was unconscious, along with my wallet.

The lights went off in the living room and then a single light came on in the room I had woken in earlier. I could make out two figures. One was the tattooed man. The other was Molly. Then they moved out of sight, and I couldn't see anyone. I stared at that window for two or three hours, before the light was switched off and everything went dark.

I must have dropped off eventually, but it was a frenzied sleep.

The heat woke me. I was lying on the foam rubber. There was no sound from the house. The dogs were still in their crate. There was no way I could get free. The leg iron was locked tight and the chain was welded to the stake.

There had to be a way out of this. Maybe it was just some crazy game and, when they'd had their fun, we'd be let go?

But that was bullshit, I knew. They wouldn't let us go; however, they hadn't killed us yet. I decided that they must want us alive, at least for a while, but sometime they'd kill us.

The back door opened and Lila walked into the yard. She was wearing a white top and Molly's floral skirt. She was a similar build and colouring to Molly and would have been quite pretty if she cleaned herself up a bit. A few decent feeds and a shampoo would do wonders for her. She carried a tin bowl with scraps for the dogs. The dogs jumped to attention.

'What about me?' I asked. 'Do I get to eat, or is starvation part of the game?'

'This *is* for you—and the dogs,' she said, and she hurled the contents of the bowl towards us. Half-eaten, half-burnt ribs and corn landed on the ground. The dogs went straight for them.

'How am I supposed to eat any of that shit? The dogs'll rip me to bits.'

'That's life,' came a voice from the doorway. It was the guy who'd hit me. 'You better find a way. You'll need the energy. Tommy's got some heavy work planned for you, man!'

Tommy must be the tattooed man.

'C'mon, Lila,' the guy said. 'What about *our* breakfast?'

'Fuck off, Lee, I'll get it when I'm ready.'

Then Lila turned to me: 'You'd better eat or you'll die, Mister.'

'I'll die anyway, won't I, Lila?'

'Stop talking, Lila, and get inside.'

It was Tommy. He stood in the doorway wearing jeans with no shirt or shoes. He looked strong. He smiled at me. 'Pretty wife.'

He smiled again. And they all went back into the house. I wanted to kill them. I especially wanted to kill Tommy.

The morning passed. I longed to see Molly, but I saw no one. My mind focused on survival.

The yard was a mess; overgrown and cluttered. A couple of old cars were slowly dying beyond the dog box. Rusted chains and tyres littered the area. A late-model Chevrolet pick-up was parked near the back door and reminded me that the rental car was nowhere to be seen. I wondered if the car rental company would expect me to repay the cost of the car. How weird our minds can be.

I was hungry by now; very hungry. A couple of the ribs lay beyond the dog's reach. I grabbed them up. They tasted horrible, but I had to stay strong.

One of the dogs had been feasting on a large bone, but it was now resting. The other dog, which had obviously been biding its time, went for the bone, and then it was on. Don't ask me what breed they were; I've never been overly fond of dogs. I find them stupid.

Finally the dog that wanted the bone pinned the other down and sank its teeth into the conquered dog's throat. It was a show of strength. It barely broke skin but showed it could if it wished. The other dog went limp and, when released, skulked away and lay quiet. I was fascinated.

The fight had obviously stirred the house into some sort of action. Voices were raised, but only the men's voices. Next minute, Lee and Jerry came out. Jerry held a rifle.

Lee unlocked the leg iron. 'Get a move on, you've got work to do.'

Lee pushed me past the dogs and old cars. There was a track.

I turned.

'Follow that track,' shouted Jerry, 'and don't do anything stupid.'

I wanted to ask about Molly but held off. We followed the track for about a hundred metres and came into a clearing. Before me, in various states of undress, were more cars— very expensive, very modern cars.

With Palm Springs just down the road, it became clear what was on: these men were stealing cars and bringing them here to be stripped or sold, or both. There must have been about twelve in the clearing, and another ten or so rusted chassis lay beyond them. A dilapidated shed housed a red Porsche with a couple of panels missing and the hood up.

A new shed was being constructed next to it. A slab had been laid and a large post stood at each corner. There were sheets of galvanised iron stacked nearby with various lengths of cut wood piled beside. This, no doubt, was what I was to work on.

Lee brought a toolbox from the shed and went back for an electric saw. Jerry sat under the shade of a tree, feet up on the front bumper of a black Mercedes Sports.

For the next two hours I cut wood and drilled holes as directed by Jerry. There was no slacking. Lee, meanwhile, continued to strip the Porsche, relieving it of its sound system, lights and doors.

'About bloody time!'

I wondered what Jerry was talking about, but I was too buggered to turn around.

'We were busy.'

It was Tommy's voice. He laughed. As I turned, I saw Molly was with him, holding a plate of sandwiches. Lila carried a sixpack of beer.

Molly looked washed out. She was wearing a light dress. It was grubby and it wasn't hers; it was tight on her. She looked like a whore, that's the first thing I thought. Her hair was unbrushed and her bra straps showed. She looked straight at me; as far as I could tell they hadn't beaten her. At least she was alive, I thought. I didn't want to consider anything else that might have happened to her.

Lila handed the sixpack to Jerry. He threw a beer to Lee. The sandwiches were put on the bonnet of the Merc.

I walked towards the car.

'No, no, no,' said Tommy. 'You get fed later. Back to work.'

'I'm hungry.'

'Back to work.'

I hated the bastard, but I wasn't going to waste my energy arguing.

Molly never spoke.

I continued working up on the roof for the rest of the afternoon, nailing the rafters in place, while the others all sat around joking and drinking. Lila was definitely Jerry's girl, but Lee had the hots for her, it was obvious.

Tommy had taken from the Porsche a contraption that turned out to be a crossbow. It looked new and I suspected that he'd got it by mail order from one of those survivalist magazines. He kept shooting at a cut-out figure of Saddam Hussein nailed to the side of the old shed.

'Here, have a go, pretty wife.'

I looked down. Tommy had given the crossbow to Molly.

'I'd rather not,' she said.

'I said, have a go.'

Tommy moved behind her. He knew I was looking. He put his arms around her, lifting the bow to face height. His head was alongside Molly's.

'Now, pull the trigger.'

Molly pulled the trigger. She closed her eyes as she fired.

'One dead Saddam! Nice shot.'

Molly opened her eyes. There was an arrow between Hussein's eyes.

Tommy looked at me. 'A lady of many talents,' he laughed.

I felt I couldn't take anymore. I was about to hurl the hammer at this piece of scum when a cry of pain erupted from Lee.

'Fuckin' tooth!' he yelled. 'Christ, a filling's dropped out!'

Everyone looked at him.

'Poor baby's got a toothache!'

'Shut your fuckin' mouth, Lila.'

Jerry stood up and walked towards Lee. 'What did ya say, prick?'

'I've gotta fuckin hole in my tooth and it fuckin hurts.'

As he spoke, Lee was backing off fast.

'Apologise, prick!' Jerry said as he kept moving towards Lee.

'Sit down and shut up, both of you.'

Tommy had spoken.

Molly then said something to Tommy. I couldn't make it out.

'No kiddin?' He looked at me. 'Hey, you a dentist?'

'Yes,' I replied, looking straight at Molly.

'Get down here!' he ordered.

I told Lee to sit down. He sat on the bonnet of the Merc. 'Show me.'

He opened his mouth. I doubt he'd ever cleaned his teeth. Funny thing was, they were strong white teeth with only a couple of fillings. And he was right—one had dropped out.

'Got any gum?' I asked Tommy.

He passed me a piece.

I gave it to Lee: 'Chew on this for a while.'

Lee chewed. I took a bit and jammed it in the hole.

'Don't talk for a while. Let it get hard. Should do the trick.'

'You mean this'll stop the pain?'

'The cold beer probably hit a nerve after you lost the filling. If it's not abscessed, you'll be okay till you get to a dentist in town.'

Tommy put his crossbow back in the Porsche and gave orders to finish up. He walked off with his arm around Molly's waist. If I didn't die here, I vowed, I would kill him.

Tommy stopped and yelled back: 'Do a check around, Lee. I don't want anyone out there looking for our friends.'

When we got back to the house, Lee took one of the dogs and went off in the Chev. As the truck took off, a back tyre shot a tangled piece of wire across the yard. It landed right near me. No one noticed.

Jerry leg-ironed me.

'What about some food?' I asked.

'That's between you and Mickey, I'd reckon.'

I looked at Jerry.

'The dog,' explained Lila. Then they both walked into the house.

I lay down on the foam rubber. Dusk was setting in. I lay thinking.

As night came in, I kept looking at Mickey. He was the stronger of the two dogs. He lay sleeping; he was on his own. I zeroed in on him. It was he who would determine whether I'd eat later.

The piece of wire was nearby. I reached for it, untangled it. Then I looked at Mickey again. His back legs lay across his chain. I had to stay strong if there was any chance of getting through this alive.

Music and laughter came from the house. Molly stood at the lighted window. She was smiling. Molly was enjoying this. Of course, she'd find this exciting. Danger always excited her.

My mind was a mess. What was I thinking? But why wasn't she trying to get away? She certainly had no leg iron.

It was now or never. I lifted myself off the foam. Slowly, I moved towards Mickey.

Now I was within his chain's length. I stopped. Mickey was still out to it. I crept forward. I stood over the dog.

As if he sensed me there, he opened his eyes. I quickly wrapped the wire around his jaw and then the chain around his back legs.

He struggled and fought to get up on his free legs. But I was on his back, pulling the wire tight and wrapping the chain around him.

Finally, he was bound tight. Then I turned him over to face me. 'Okay, Mickey, I eat tonight.'

And then I sank my teeth into his neck. He struggled. I bit down until I could taste blood. He went limp. I looked into his eyes. He stared at me and started to whimper.

Finally I undid the chain and took the wire from his jaws. This was the moment of truth. He got to his feet, looked at me. I held my ground. And then he skulked off to his crate.

I had won. I went back to my bed and waited.

The night wore on, as did the revelry in the house. Then the back door opened and Lila came out with supper. A bucket of scraps was hurled into the yard. Lila looked at me and smiled, then turned and went back inside.

Someone had cooked up a storm. Partly eaten T-bones, potatoes, tomatoes and mushrooms were being gulped down by Mickey. I walked towards the food. Mickey stopped. He began to growl. I growled back and stared into his eyes. I picked up a bone. Mickey looked at me; then, head down, he kept eating.

That night Mickey and I filled up. Sometime later in

the night I was aware of Lee returning to chain up the second dog.

The slamming of the back door woke me. Molly and Lila came out giggling together like a couple of twin sisters. Both had washed their hair and were towelling it dry in the sun. Molly now wore cut-off jeans and Lila was in Molly's swimsuit. It was as if they'd swapped identities.

There was a forty-four-gallon drum full of water near the stairs. They began to flick water at each other. The sun was hot and I wished some water would come my way.

The three men came outside and sat on the stairs watching the girls. Molly's T-shirt was soaked and you could see the outline of her breasts through it. The men were obviously enjoying the sight.

Tommy got up and walked over to me, grabbed my hair, and said, 'Up we get.'

I resisted and he punched me in the side of the head. It hurt. 'Up! Now!'

Lee came over and unlocked the leg iron. The others watched. Tommy marched me to the drum, still holding my hair.

'I can see you need cooling down.'

He shoved my head into the drum. I thought this might be it. And, anyway, why not?

Tommy's grip was strong. I began to struggle. The seconds passed. He was obviously going to drown me. My lungs were bursting. He continued to hold me down. I became drowsy, and then suddenly he pulled me from the drum and threw me to the ground.

The three men laughed as I fought for air. I lay on the ground. I couldn't look at anyone, especially not Molly.

'Now, get him to work.'

Tommy went inside. I got up as Lee and Jerry came over. Out of the corner of my eye I could see Molly and Lila drying themselves off. Molly was staring at me.

The rest of the day was spent putting up the framework for the shed. The rental car appeared and was stripped clean by Jerry and Lee.

Late in the afternoon, I noticed Mickey digging around near the back of the old shed. An area had recently been ploughed and a tractor sat idle nearby. I was getting the roofing iron ready when Mickey came up and dropped a bone he'd found in front of me.

I looked down at the bone. Five years at university for dentistry had taught me plenty about the human body and I recognised the bone. It was a fibula, one of the two bones between the knee and ankle.

Now I knew. They didn't just bring cars back here to be stripped; sometimes they brought the owners. But when the cars left, the owners stayed. That was what was in store for us—or, more accurately, for me. Molly seemed to have cast in her lot with these killers now.

There was maybe two more days work to go on the shed. What then?

I slept uneasily that night.

Next morning work started early. Something was on. Most of the roof was battened down by late afternoon. Lila brought more beer for Lee and Jerry. She still wore the swimsuit. She knew she looked good in it. Lee couldn't take his eyes off her.

Jerry went to the house for a new drill. Lee was drinking pretty heavily. He started to come on to Lila. She didn't exactly tell him to piss off. Lee put one arm around her and his other hand on her arse.

Lila tried to pull away, but Lee wouldn't let go. Next thing I knew, Lee was on the ground and Jerry was kicking the shit out of him.

As drunk as Lee was, he still managed to get himself up and grab Jerry by the throat. They grappled with each other, punching and shoving until they were both on the ground, rolling against the front wheels of the Merc. Jerry got on top of Lee and started smashing him in the face.

An arrow flew between their heads, landing in the Merc's front tyre. The two men froze. Tommy stood with Molly. He was holding the crossbow.

'Ease up, boys. This is not a good idea. This is a very bad idea.'

Jerry and Lee got up off the ground.

'Jerry and Lila, get into town—you know what we're after. Lee, lock him up.'

Jerry and Lila took off, clearly set on another steal.

Molly and Tommy headed back to the house.

That night came in quieter than past nights; no raised voices, no laughter. Then Tommy came into the yard. He unlocked the leg iron.

'Inside!'

Molly was sitting at the kitchen table opposite Lee. Lee was holding his jaw.

'I thought you were a dentist,' Lee said.

I didn't reply.

'So why is this pain fuckin killing me?'

'I guess you've got an abscess.'

'Take the tooth out,' said Tommy.

'You got any pliers?' I asked.

Tommy looked to Molly: 'Under the sink.'

Molly began looking. The cupboard was a mess. Molly took out a tin of paint stripper and behind it lay the pliers.

'Got any gin?' I asked.

Lee went to the other room and came back with a bottle.

'Get as much of that into you as possible.'

He started drinking.

After about twenty minutes, I said, 'Okay, open up.'

I told Tommy to hold Lee steady. Lee was drunk by now.

I got the pliers around the tooth then pulled. It hurt, no doubt about it.

'Hurry it up,' said Tommy.

'It's a tough tooth to pull. Hold him tight.'

Lee's pain made me feel good. I took my time. Finally I yanked it hard. Lee screamed. Out came the tooth.

'Drink some more,' I said.

Lee would be out cold very soon.

'Back outside,' Tommy said to me. Then he turned to Molly. 'You'd better join us.'

Molly watched as Tommy locked me up. I watched Molly.

When they went back into the house, I lay down on the foam rubber. Across from me lay Mickey. He was awake, just watching. Probably hungry too, I thought. The other dog must have gone with Jerry and Lila. I guessed Mickey was Tommy's dog.

Then an almighty scream made Mickey and me jump. The back door crashed open and Molly came rushing into the yard. She was holding the key to the leg iron.

'I threw paint stripper in his eyes. He's blind.'

She let me loose.

'What now?' she said.

I couldn't think. I needed answers, but the questions were all jumbled.

'What now?' Molly yelled. 'Lee's out to it. I don't know how long Tommy's going to be blind, and the others are away. What do we do?'

I grabbed her arm and steered her down the moonlit track.

At the sheds I pointed to the Porsche. 'Get in.'

There were a few jerry cans of petrol in the old shed, so I grabbed one and threw it into the back of the car.

I had no idea if the car would start. I turned the key. The engine burst into life. I gunned the Porsche down the track and screamed past the house.

Tommy was at the door, his hands over his eyes. He was screaming. 'You bitch! You won't get away from me! I'll get you!'

We careered out of the gate. The road we'd come in on continued past the house. Which way to go?

We chose to go deeper into the bush. So long as the road wasn't a dead end.

It wasn't.

We drove on in silence for over an hour. My heart was beating furiously. The Porsche wasn't built for bush tracks. Even though I pushed it, we'd have been lucky to have gone ten miles by now.

Where were we? I hadn't a clue. The thing that worried me was there had been no turn-offs. If they were looking for us, they'd be on the same track. I wanted them to believe we'd headed for Palm Springs.

We continued on for another half hour or so. The scrub grew sparser and at last we spotted a side track. I turned down it. About a kilometre ahead was the beginning of a small mountain range. Maybe we could hide there for the rest of the night.

If our lives hadn't been at stake, the drive would have been strangely beautiful. The moon was high and full, and the rocky outcrops and distant gorges looked bold and eerie.

We drove along a small stream that flowed silver and reached the safety of the rocks. There was something of a track going up into the range. We took it. A mile in, we stopped. We could see back to the road. We'd know if the men were following.

The hours passed. Molly told me what had happened. After I'd pulled Lee's tooth and was locked up, Molly and Tommy had something to eat. Lee crashed in his room— World War III wouldn't have woken him. Molly and Tommy had gone into the bedroom. I tried to stay focused as she told me her story.

As Tommy got into bed, Molly said she'd like a gin. It was still in the kitchen. Tommy normally never let Molly out of his sight.

Molly went to the kitchen and poured the paint stripper into a glass. She walked back into the bedroom and over to the bed. She sat on the bed alongside Tommy. She smiled at him. He smiled back. She leaned into him and threw the paint stripper into his eyes. All hell broke loose. She grabbed Tommy's pants off the floor, got the key and raced out to me.

There was much more I wanted to ask her. It was strange; I felt I was with a different woman. This wasn't the woman I'd known for twenty years: the woman who'd taken the kids to school each day when they were young; who'd cooked Christmas dinner and spent weeks getting everyone's Christmas presents right; the woman who got into bed with me every night and read and asked me about the workings of the world.

But, then, I wasn't that man anymore either. What would happen to us if we got out of this?

The moon started to fade and the sun started to come up. It was about an hour into the daylight when we saw the dust. There were two vehicles. I could make out the Chevy truck, and an old Dodge that I'd previously seen out the back.

They stopped.

Tommy and Lee got out and talked.

Then they got back into the cars.

I watched the Dodge continue along the road. The Chevy was heading towards us. I started the Porsche and moved off quietly. The road kept going up. The Chevy was at the foot of the mountain. They probably knew every possible place you could drive to around here.

I turned the wheel and stopped.

I looked across at Molly and then backed up.

'David, what are you doing?'

I straightened the car. We were now facing down the track.

I got out of the Porsche. 'You drive.'

I grabbed the jerry can from behind the seat.

'Drive down? Back towards them?' she asked.

'Yes, and take it easy.'

I ripped the sleeve off my shirt. Molly moved into the driver's seat. I opened the can and pushed the sleeve into the opening. Then, getting back in the car, I pressed the cigarette lighter.

'Let's go! Gun it!'

Molly planted it. Whoever was in the Chevy must have heard us. He didn't know we were coming down, though. I grabbed the cigarette lighter and held it to the shirt. It scorched, then lit.

Now the Chevy could see us. It was Tommy. We were charging at each other. Molly looked to me and gritted her teeth.

Tommy leaned out the window, smiling. He was holding a rifle. The first couple of shots hit the ground in front of us. Then he grabbed the wheel with both hands. We were about twenty yards apart.

'At the last minute, swerve to the left to pass him,' I yelled.

Molly stared straight ahead, gripping the wheel; her knuckles were white.

Tommy leaned out the window and fired again. A bullet hit the frame of the car and ricocheted off.

Molly swerved. I hurled the can into the back of the truck as it passed. The sleeve was flaming. Tommy looked back at us and into the tray of the truck.

He opened the door and was in the air going over the cliff as the truck exploded alongside him.

We didn't stop.

At the foot of the mountain we did stop.

We were alive.

We hugged each other savagely.

We flew from LA to Sydney two days later. The police had taken our statements and were considerate of our desire to get home.

We didn't speak much on the flight.

A few months later a letter from the LA Police Department thanked Molly and me for our help in uncovering a ring of car thieves.

A number of human remains had been found on the property where we were held and were being identified.

I'm back to being a dentist. It's not so bad. Even enjoying looking in mouths. Don't like pulling teeth, though.

Molly is still in publishing, but also writing a book. We've never spoken about our ordeal.

We both wake with nightmares now and again. But that's okay, because they're *only* nightmares.

BE NOT AFRAID

Paul Madden sat and stared. How many times had he done this?

A lot.

But it was different today.

He was alone. It wasn't Sunday.

A sign out front said: ALL WELCOME. SIT OR PRAY. GOD IS HERE FOR YOU.

Paul had always found the cross with Jesus nailed to it fascinating. It sat above the altar.

He had been coming to this church for twenty-four years. Ever since he decided Hannah would make her First Communion. She was about to transfer to a Catholic girls' school after two years at the local public school around the corner from where they lived, and it sort of helped if the kids were practising Catholics.

The practising didn't last long.

By the time Hannah was twelve she had stopped going to church. But Paul kept going.

He liked the humility of the parishioners.

That's all. The humility.

As he stared at the cross, Paul Madden couldn't help wondering what Mary and Joseph must have been thinking as they saw their son hanging from the nails smashed into his hands and feet.

The pain they must have felt.

Paul felt pain.

Hannah had been found dead in her bed three weeks ago.

Alone.

An empty bottle of sleeping tablets on her side table.

With a glass and half-full bottle of riesling.

The police had investigated and concluded it was death by suicide.

No suspicious circumstances.

Paul's marriage had wandered away some time ago.

Irene and he were never really suited, but it'd suited them both to get married.

Time had been passing for both of them and they'd been seeing each other for around three months.

So why not?

She didn't love him.

And Paul didn't love Irene.

But a couple of years later along came beautiful Hannah.

So that made it official: they were a family.

They stayed a family until Hannah's last year of high school.

The parting had been harder than Paul thought it would be.

He'd grown accustomed to being a part of something, even though he'd known that that something wasn't going to last.

Irene moved on.

Paul moved on.

Hannah closed shop for a while. For a good couple of years.

She did a business degree at Sydney Uni then joined McGregors, an accountancy firm. She did well there and became a senior manager. Had continued working at the firm up until three weeks ago.

———

'You make me happy. So happy. It won't always be like this, will it?'

'You know it won't. Thank you for understanding. I know it's difficult.'

'Can you stay?'

———

Paul Madden sat across from Sergeant Harmon, the cop handling Hannah's death.

He didn't look like a cop.

Be lucky to be five foot eight. And a boy.

When did it all change? When did cops stop looking like cops?

'How can I help you, Mr Madden?'

'You can't. I'm not really sure why I'm here, Sergeant.'

'I do understand how difficult this must be for you, Mr Madden.'

Paul Madden looked at the cop on the other side of the desk. He asked for a glass of water.

The sergeant poured him a glass from a jug on the desk.

'Thank you.'

Paul Madden drank from the glass. He hadn't realised he was so thirsty.

He finished his water and placed the glass back on the desk.

Sergeant Harmon opened the cabinet behind him and removed a box.

'These are some of Hannah's personal effects and her computer, Mr Madden. We no longer need them.'

Paul Madden looked at the box and then at the cop.

'I don't believe Hannah killed herself.'

Hannah's funeral took place at the Eastern Suburbs Memorial Park in Matraville.

Matraville used to be the working-class brother of Maroubra in the sixties.

Maroubra had a beach. Matraville didn't.

Matraville was where Paul grew up.

Lots of housing commission homes there and Dot and Fred, Paul's parents, had one.

Dot was a bookkeeper and Fred a toolmaker.

Paul used to help his mum with the bookkeeping. He got pretty good at it. Probably why he became an accountant.

And he's probably why Hannah became an accountant.

They said goodbye to Hannah in the South Chapel.

Paul spoke. Said what a lovely daughter Hannah was.

Tried to hold back the tears. But when the casket was lowered into the ground he broke down. Bawled his eyes out.

Fifteen people signed the book. He knew none of them. It seemed like there were two groups. The biggest was obviously from McGregors.

Irene was there too. She'd flown down from the Gold Coast, where she'd moved after the divorce. Said she needed to be somewhere sunny.

Irene and Hannah weren't close. Never had been.

Maybe Irene always knew she didn't belong.

Or didn't want to belong.

Or maybe she knew the hurt that was coming and was just looking after herself.

Who knows what goes on in the human heart?

The following week Paul cleaned out Hannah's apartment.

She'd bought a one-bedroom in Petersham, one of those inner-city suburbs everyone has heard of without being exactly sure where it is.

Paul remembered how excited Hannah was to move there.

She'd been saving relentlessly for a deposit and had finally been approved for a mortgage and now she had her own place.

She'd been staying with Paul in Rozelle, another inner-city suburb of Sydney. They'd hired a ute and carted her stuff over there one Saturday afternoon.

'The start of my adult life,' Hannah told Paul as they carried her boxes inside.

And now Paul stood in the same apartment ten years later looking at the bed where Hannah's adult life had ended.

––––

'Will you come over or shall we meet somewhere?'

'Better I come over. You know how it is.'

'I could come to you. I don't mind.'

'No. I'll come over. Okay?'

'Yep. You come over. I'll be here.'

––––

Paul gave all Hannah's furniture and clothes to the St Vincent de Paul at Rozelle.

They were very grateful.

She'd left behind a few files. Some to do with work obviously, and other stuff.

Paul thought he'd go through it all slowly.

Didn't know when he'd start, but he wanted to know his daughter's life.

Even a little bit.

To understand why she had ended her life.

Her so-young life.

Hannah was a quiet girl. Didn't share a lot. Spoke about work a bit. Accountancy work. The ethics of it. Her private life she kept private.

Paul Madden had been just eighteen when he received the letter.

He'd known what it was.

Paul had gone with Dot and Fred to The Entrance for the Easter holidays.

The Entrance was a small surfing and fishing village on the coast about a two-hour drive north of Sydney.

They had been going there every Easter. This was their tenth year.

It had changed over the past sixty years. Like everything.

More houses. More people.

Back then you went out in the morning and your parents didn't see you until dinner time.

Paul had known this would be the last time he'd be going to The Entrance with his parents. He'd just taken a job with an accountancy firm and was studying at the same time. But now he was holding a letter that could change his life.

Dot and Fred watched as Paul read the letter marked *Official* from the Australian government.

'I'm in. Have to report for a medical next week.'

Dot started to cry.

Fred put his arm around Paul's shoulder. 'Can you ask for a deferment?'

'Maybe. But I don't want a deferment. I want to do my duty. Gotta stop the commies.'

So Paul went to Vietnam as a conscript.

The regulars looked down on conscripts, but once action happened they were all soldiers and reliant on each other.

On Paul's first assignment, moving slowly through the Vietnamese forests, his mate Charlie Neill turned and gave Paul a smile. Action at last, that smile said. Charlie had been desperate to get out and get among it. He was a conscript but intended to enlist after the war.

Later, Charlie's smile ended up all over Paul's face.

A sniper's bullet went straight through Charlie's head, exploding it onto Paul.

Blood and pieces of meat and skull.

Charlie no longer existed.

Paul came back from Vietnam when the prime minister withdrew Australia's troops.

Paul thought he had been fighting for his country, but upon his return he found he was regarded as no hero. The country was anti the war and anti anyone who had participated in it.

Paul remembered his mate Charlie.

It could have been Charlie who came back and Paul who had his head blown off.

Paul had nightmares.

How could you not?

Paul never spoke of his time in Vietnam.

Not to anyone.

Dot or Fred or Irene or Hannah.

He compartmentalised it. Shoved the experience into a box and shoved it into the back of his mind somewhere.

Never to be opened.

Paul stood waiting in reception at McGregors. The company had been founded by Hamish McGregor AM, a very prominent name in Sydney society.

Paul had an appointment with Terry Marr, Hannah's boss.

'Mr Madden.'

Terry Marr was dressed in a suit with an open-necked shirt. Checked. He should have been the cop.

Six foot at least and, if not exactly handsome, certainly with presence and an English accent.

He led Paul past a number of desks and into his office.

Everyone knew he was Hannah's father and they watched him as he passed by.

Terry Marr sat on his side of the desk, Paul Madden opposite.

'Thanks for seeing me.'

'We are so saddened here at McGregors, Mr Madden. Hannah was loved by us all.'

Paul turned to look at the open-plan office outside.

Many eyes were on him. Sad faces. They all knew more about Hannah and her life than he did. What made her laugh. How good she was at her work. Who she was close to.

'I came to collect her things, Mr Marr.'

Terry Marr picked up his phone and asked someone to bring in Hannah's belongings.

'There is very little here, I'm afraid. The police took a fair bit, including Hannah's files and computer.'

A young woman brought in a box and placed it on the desk in front of Paul.

'I'm so sorry for your loss, Mr Madden. My name is Lizzie and I was a friend of Hannah's. I will miss her. We all will.'

Paul nodded. 'You were at the funeral. I recognise you. Thank you, Lizzie.'

Lizzie left the office.

'I didn't make it to the funeral unfortunately,' Terry Marr said. 'I was called out of town.'

Paul Madden nodded. 'Mr Marr, it's hard for me to believe Hannah took her own life. How was she during the weeks before . . . before she . . . you know? Did she appear upset or distressed?'

'No, Mr Madden, we were all taken totally by surprise. Hannah was always such an even-tempered girl. Never one to cause problems. She always seemed at ease and on top of things. She was immensely liked.

'I only got to know her in the past year, when I moved to Sydney, but like everyone else I was very fond of Hannah.'

'Can I see her desk?'

'Of course.'

Terry Marr led Paul Madden to a desk by the window. Hannah's desk.

'Great view,' Paul Madden said, and then he looked to Terry Marr. 'I'm sorry. Stupid thing to say. Forgive me.'

From Hannah's desk you could see clear over Circular Quay and down the harbour.

A view Hannah would never see again. Why had she never spoken to her father about her office view?

There was so much Paul Madden didn't know about his daughter's life.

Well, that was about to change.

'Is there anything more I can help you with, Mr Madden?' Terry Marr asked.

Paul Madden shook his head.

'Please call if I can help.'

'Thank you, I will.'

Paul Madden sat on a bench with a view of those entering and leaving the office building in which McGregors was located. Constructed in the sixties, it was named after one of the big insurance companies. The insurance company no longer occupied the whole building. It now had offices out in the suburbs, where most of Sydney lived.

It was only two in the afternoon.

He doubted employees from McGregors would be leaving before five thirty.

But Paul Madden was good at waiting.

He'd learnt that as a conscript.

Slow, silent movements.

As though you were never moving.

Sitting and waiting was easy.

———

Lizzie walked out of the office block at 6.15 pm.

'Excuse me, Lizzie!'

'Oh! Hi, Mr Madden.' She stopped as Paul Madden stepped up to her. 'Can I help you?'

'Do you think, Lizzie, that we could sit somewhere, grab a coffee? I would love to ask you a bit about Hannah.'

Lizzie looked at Hannah's dad.

She could see the pain and need in his face.

'Sure.'

She led him to a small cafe on the Quay.

'How can I help, Mr Madden?'

'Please call me Paul.'

'Okay, Paul.'

They ordered coffees.

He told her that, even though he and his daughter loved each other, there had not been a lot of personal communication between the two of them.

He hoped that hearing about Hannah—even little things—would help him to understand why she took her life.

'Hannah was very funny,' Lizzie said. 'Often came out with the unexpected. Never nasty funny, but sort of darkly wry. If you know what I mean.'

Paul smiled.

'She was conscientious. Took her job very seriously. Wouldn't leave for lunch or would sometimes forget to eat if she was absorbed in work.'

'Did she talk about boyfriends?'

'No. She did join in conversations about men, but she never spoke about men in her life.'

'Do you think there *were* men in Hannah's life, Lizzie?'

'I don't know.'

Lizzie sat back in her chair and looked once again at Paul.

There sure was pain in that face. But was it because of Hannah, or had it been there for a long time?

'There was a time a couple of years back,' Lizzie said. 'McGregors flew a number of us to the Gold Coast for a three-day weekend. About ten of us seniors. It was meant to be a sort of company retreat.

'You know, we'd discuss the philosophy of the company and that kind of thing. But we had fun dinners and hit the bars, too. The Gold Coast is great for bars.

'I remember, when we came back, Hannah was really quite different for a few weeks. Really, really happy. And wearing lipstick and new outfits. I mean, she always looked stylish, but she started really glamming up.

'Then all of a sudden that ended and it was back to the Hannah we were used to. We all teased her a bit about a boyfriend, but she laughed it off.'

The two of them sat there in silence, looking out at the harbour.

'Was there ever anything else like that, Lizzie? Anything out of the ordinary?'

Not that Lizzie could remember.

She thanked Paul for the coffee and explained she had to leave.

Yoga class.

As she got up from her chair she turned to him. 'There was a time about four months ago. I went into the ladies' room at the office just before lunch and found Hannah in there. It was obvious she had been crying.

'I asked if I could help. She told me no and said she would be out for the rest of the afternoon. That was a Thursday, and in fact she didn't return until Monday. It was strange for Hannah. She was never sick.'

'And how was she on the Monday?' Paul Madden asked.

Lizzie tried to recall. 'Subdued,' she said. 'Subdued for the rest of that week. Anyway, I really do have to go.'

'Will you take my number, please, in case you think of anything that . . . well, you know.'

Paul handed Lizzie his card.

Lizzie put it in her bag.

'Bye, Paul. I'm dreadfully sorry.'

Lizzie walked out of the coffee shop and onto the street.

Paul Madden stayed at the coffee shop looking out at the harbour.

———

The two soldiers were deactivating the mines that surrounded the camp, protecting it overnight.

It was now morning.

Soldiers who were finishing their duty were never sent out on missions for the four or five days before they flew out. They'd done their bit and were to be looked after for these last days. Same with deactivating.

It was a no-no for these soldiers.

But an American captain was in charge of the camp and he'd decided these two soldiers should do the deactivating. Some of the Australian soldiers in the camp objected, but the captain wouldn't have any of it: 'This is my camp. You'll do as I say.'

The explosion woke Paul Madden.

He was screaming and in a sweat.

Wringing wet.

He sat up in bed.

The lid of the box was opening.

'Bless me, Father, for I have sinned. It's been many years since my last confession.'

Paul Madden hadn't been inside a confessional since he was a kid. But he knew he needed help.

'How can I help you?' the priest asked.

Paul was silent.

'How can I help you, my son?'

'I don't know that you can, Father.'

'Go on,' said the priest.

'My daughter has died and I'm worried that the anger inside me will cause me to hurt someone.'

'Did you love your daughter?'

'Of course.'

'That's all that matters. She is with God now.'

Paul was silent.

The priest was silent too.

'I have darkness inside me, Father. Darkness that wants to come out. Bless me, Father, and pray for me.'

At that, Paul Madden rose and walked from the confessional.

Three boxes faced him. They were on the floor in front of the television.

Where should he start?

Paul Madden took Hannah's computer from the box the cop had given him and sat it on the carpet.

The police had attached a note to the computer with the password '*agnes*'. It was Irene's middle name.

Also in the box was a diary.

A calendar that Paul recognised as having come from Hannah's fridge.

The empty bottle of sleeping pills.

Some other prescription drugs.

Paul imagined that the apartment had been dusted for prints and searched thoroughly.

There was a work Filofax, which must have been fifteen years old.

A bunch of A4 sheets. Some folded. Paul recognised Hannah's writing.

The cops must have kept any work files and returned them to McGregors.

There was a copy of the coroner's report.

Paul studied it. He read that sleeping pills had been in Hannah's system. Alcohol too.

Paul looked at the bottle of sleeping pills.

The prescribing doctor was not the family doctor that Paul and Hannah had seen forever. When did she change doctors?

The box from McGregors contained bugger-all.

Spare change.

Matches.

A fountain pen given to Hannah by Paul on her first day of work. It had never been used.

Paul felt his emotions rise.

He was pleased she had kept it all these years.

There was a photo of Hannah and Paul taken at a school prize giving.

And one of Irene and Hannah from when Hannah was about three.

Another framed photo was obviously of work colleagues.

Paul recognised Lizzie and Terry Marr.

The picture had been taken at a restaurant.

The third box contained things Paul had gathered from Hannah's apartment.

There were five books that Hannah had loved.

The first *Harry Potter*. She adored Harry Potter.

Little Women by Louisa May Alcott. Hannah had been obsessed by it.

Moby Dick. Paul could never understand what Hannah responded to in such a strange tale.

Alice in Wonderland had been around forever. It had been read and reread by Hannah for the past twenty years.

And *The Complete Works of Shakespeare*. She had always been a Shakespeare nut.

Paul Madden smiled at the memory. Hannah had read *Romeo and Juliet* to him over one weekend long ago.

There was a pair of rosary beads.

Some jewellery. Hannah wasn't big on jewellery.

Postcards from friends and family.

Paul looked at the postcards.

He had sent a few from business trips. The Pacific Islands, the UK and the USA.

Irene had sent some silly Gold Coast postcards. All wishing you were here.

There were a number of bankcards and credit cards and receipts and club memberships.

And one small card that Paul hadn't seen before. It was about the same size as a credit card, but cardboard.

The front of the card had just the letters *AA*.

And on the back was a phone number.

'Hello. I'm Paul Madden. I think you knew my daughter Hannah.'

Paul had the phone in one hand and the AA card in the other. He sat on his bed.

There was silence from the other end of the phone.

'Hello? Are you there?'

'Yes, I'm here. What do you want, Mr Madden?'

Paul explained that he was just after a few answers.

That he loved his daughter and was having a hard time believing she took her own life.

'I don't think I can help you, Mr Madden.'

'Please. I don't even know your name, but please, sir, can we not meet and talk?'

There was silence again.

Paul waited.

'Mr Madden, you do know what AA stands for, I guess. It's Alcoholics Anonymous.

'Hannah had a little trouble with alcohol at times.

'I was her sponsor. When and where would you like to meet?'

'It's my fault. I know. I should have been more careful.'

'These things happen.'

'What will I do?'

'Leave it with me. I'll get a name.'

———

They were sitting on the verandah of the London Hotel in Balmain. Another inner-city suburb, this one known for its musos and artists—although the last ten years had made it too pricey for most musos and artists, and a fair few others.

Hannah's sponsor was Scott Freestone.

A muso.

And, of course, an alcoholic.

Been sober for fifteen years.

'I didn't know Hannah was an alcoholic, Scott.'

Scott was drinking lemon, lime and bitters. He raised his glass to Paul Madden. 'I could give up the grog, but not pubs. Cheers.' They sat looking out at Darling Street.

'Hannah came to a meeting in Glebe about eighteen months ago.

'She was a smart girl.

'Recognised she was going to have a problem, if she didn't already have one. Wanted to get on top of it.

'Said she was doing a bottle of wine a night. Sometimes two. It had been going on for a few months.

'Waking up on the lounge.

'Scared her.

'I offered to be her sponsor.'

'Did she say what got her drinking, Scott?'

'Not initially, no, but later I sussed it was about a bloke.'

'Do you know who?'

Scott explained that Hannah was quite private—unlike a lot in AA, who couldn't wait to tell you everything.

'She did all right. Right from the go.

'Would ring me every couple of weeks to let me know all was well.

'That went on for over a year, I think. Not always every two weeks but, you know, maybe every six weeks, couple of months.'

'And then what happened?'

Scott took a drink from his lemon, lime and bitters. He looked at Paul. 'About four months ago she told me she'd started drinking again. She was crying. I said, "Let's meet."'

Scott finished his drink. 'And?'

Scott hesitated. 'She didn't want to meet. She said she'd work it out.'

Paul told Scott that she obviously hadn't, because alcohol was found in her blood.

'That's strange. Because she rang me the week before her death and told me she'd been clean since we talked, and that she was never touching another drop.'

The two men looked at each other.

'I guess she went back to it, Scott.'

Paul Madden stepped off the plane at Coolangatta Airport and picked up a rental car. It was a forty-minute drive to the Gold Coast.

Irene had said she'd see him but couldn't pick him up.

Didn't finish work until six.

No guessing who Hannah had got her work ethic from.

Paul enjoyed the drive to Southport.

When he was a young man he'd taken this road on his way to Canungra, the army base at the back of Surfers Paradise. No paradise for the conscripts, though.

When he was an eighteen-year-old, there had been no houses along this stretch of coast. Only golden beaches.

Now house after house.

Irene lived in a tower block overlooking Southport Beach. On the fifteenth floor.

She opened the door at the first knock.

It was six thirty.

She leant into Paul and quietly embraced him. They held each other, neither speaking.

After a couple of minutes Irene straightened up, wiping her eyes. 'Our girl gone.'

Paul nodded.

Irene closed the door and led Paul inside.

'Drink?'

'Thanks.'

Paul walked out onto the balcony.

Irene took two beers from the fridge and joined him.

'Not a bad spot for a divorced woman. I get to perve on all the young surfer boys.'

She handed Paul a beer and opened the other for herself.

'You made me cry at the funeral,' she told him. 'Not that I needed help in crying.'

'But I felt your love for Hannah. You two were always close.'

'Closer than I ever was.'

They were still on the balcony.

Sitting on deckchairs now.

'That's silly. Hannah loved you. You know that.'

'Yes, I do know that, but I also know she was always more comfortable around you. That's just how it was, Paul.'

Paul looked at Irene. She was still a very attractive woman.

He hoped her life was good.

'Hannah didn't kill herself, Irene. I know it.'

Irene leant across to Paul and took his hand. 'Paul, the police investigated.'

Paul nodded his head slightly.

'Irene, I know death. Hannah didn't kill herself.'

He told her about his conversation with Lizzie. About the company get-together on the Gold Coast a couple of years earlier.

'Did Hannah contact you while she was here?'

Irene didn't answer straight away.

Then she let go of Paul's hand and sat back in the deckchair.

'Yes she did. She rang and said she had a morning free. We met for coffee. She was flying back that afternoon.'

Paul waited.

'She was in high spirits. Said they'd all had a wonderful time over the weekend. Was telling funny stories about what they'd got up to.

'I was surprised at how affectionate she was with me. She kept touching me as she was talking.

'She never used to do that with me.'

'Do you think she met someone up here?'

'She didn't say.'

'What contact have you had since then?'

'The occasional call. Just to say hello.

'Nothing special. Although on one call she seemed anxious.

'I asked her if anything was up and she said there was a big problem with a client. She hoped it would get sorted right.'

'*Get sorted right.* They were her words? Strange. Not, *Hoped it would get sorted out?*'

'No. *Get sorted right.* She brushed me off when I probed. You know what she was like when you probe. Closes down.'

Paul asked Irene when this call was.

'Just after she'd come back from her holiday to Los Angeles. Around six months ago.'

———

'I can't believe you don't have a boyfriend. What's wrong with Australian men?'

'I think it must be me. Am I boring, do you think?'

'Not that I'm noticing. I think you are very beautiful.'

'Am I blushing now?'

'Yes.'

———

The two men sat opposite each other in Terry Marr's office.

Paul had explained that he had a few more questions about Hannah and asked was it possible for them to meet again.

Terry Marr suggested he come in at the end of the office day.

It was now 6 pm and most desks were empty, but Lizzie was still beavering away at her computer by the window.

When Paul began his working life, there had been two computers. The 1401 and 1410. Both IBM. And both the size of small rooms.

What a different world it was now. Computers the size of books.

Terry Marr listened while Paul Madden spoke of Hannah's concern about a problem at the office a few months back.

She had mentioned it to her mother, Paul said. It was around the time of her return from a holiday.

'There are always work problems, Mr Madden. It's the name of the game.

'That's why we were so lucky to have Hannah at McGregors. She knew how to work through problems. One step at a time was her motto.'

'But was there a particularly difficult work situation that may have been harder than normal?' Paul asked. 'I don't want to pry into your business, but was there something around that time that rings a bell?'

Terry Marr sat and thought.

He was silent for more than a minute.

Paul waited.

Finally Terry Marr said, 'There was something that was difficult. Something Hannah unearthed on her trip to the States. We did the books for a not-for-profit company that installed solar panels. They imported the units from California for five thousand dollars apiece. After installation, they billed the government for fifty per cent of the total cost and a rebate was paid to the client. This company had been awarded a substantial grant to cover their costs, which were sizable. The administration of the grant was scrutinised and overseen by us.'

Terry Marr stopped for a moment and smiled at Paul Madden.

'As luck would have it—or bad luck would have it—Hannah decided, while she was in LA, to contact the Californian company that supplied the solar panels. She thought she would thank them and say how terrific it was that this system was so popular in Australia.

'By chance, they mentioned that the cost of the units was four thousand dollars, not five thousand.

'That meant the not-for-profit company here at home, which was getting a refund of 50 per cent of the unit price, was pocketing the difference.'

'This amounted to five hundred dollars per customer, and there had been twenty thousand customers.

'Ten million dollars of government money had gone straight into the company's coffers.'

Hannah had also found out that the Australian directors had taken the Californian company CEO and managers to Las Vegas for a long weekend, Terry Marr explained.

McGregors now knew that the Australian government was being fraudulently overcharged.

A number of discussions were held with the directors of the not-for-profit and it was decided that McGregors would no longer act for the company.

'And how did the company take that news, Mr Marr?' Paul asked.

'Not well. Its board was disbanded and a new board announced. There were some furious ex-board members.'

'And how did McGregors take it?'

'We were grateful to Hannah. I was in particular, Mr Madden. If the news of the fraud had broken while we were still dealing with the company, Hamish McGregor, my father-in-law, would have fired me and sent me packing back to England.'

'Tough is he?'

'With sons-in-law, yes. His daughter is the apple of his eye.'

'Can I ask you for the name of the company and the names of those involved?'

Terry Marr explained that this wasn't possible. He had to respect a client's privacy, even if they were no longer a client.

'I hope that answers your question, Mr Madden.'

Paul Madden shook Terry Marr's hand.

It wasn't long before Lizzie left the building.

Paul was waiting.

'Yoga on this evening?'

'No, Paul. More questions?'

They found a seat in the same coffee shop as before.

Paul asked Lizzie if she knew about the solar swindle.

Lizzie looked straight into his eyes: 'Yes, Hannah was great. She was adamant that McGregors confront the company. She could have lost her job.'

'So McGregors were loath to ask questions?'

'It was a substantial client. Worth a lot of money to us. Hannah said it was wrong what they were doing. She stood up to Terry.'

'Lizzie, would you give me the name of the company and the directors' names?'

Lizzie hesitated.

'I'm not supposed to do that. It's private company business.'

'Please, Lizzie.'

Lizzie stood up. 'I loved Hannah. She was a great girl. I'll text you.'

And then she left the coffee shop.

The address on the bottle of sleeping pills was Petersham. A Dr Rosemary Fenton.

Paul Madden had rung for an appointment.

Dr Rosemary Fenton was a large lady with kind eyes.

'Doctor, my daughter Hannah came to see you a few months back.'

The doctor looked directly into Paul Madden's eyes.

'Yes, she did, Mr Madden. The police have been in touch with a few questions. They explained to me Hannah overdosed.

'I'm very sorry for your loss. She was a lovely young woman.'

'Were you able to help the police, Dr Fenton?'

Rosemary Fenton shook her head. 'Unfortunately not. Hannah was a rather new patient. This was only her second visit.'

Paul Madden explained that he was surprised Hannah had changed doctors. She had always gone to Total Health in Balmain.

'People change doctors, Mr Madden. It's not uncommon.'

'Why did she need sleeping pills, though? I can't remember her ever using them while she lived with me.'

'I can't really help you, Mr Madden.'

'Who *can* help me, Doctor? Who can help me understand what happened to my little girl?'

Dr Fenton searched Paul Madden's face.

'Hannah was my only child. Do you have children, Dr Fenton?'

Dr Fenton waited. Thinking. Then she went to her computer, opened it and typed in a name. She turned the computer around to face Paul Madden and stepped aside. 'The doctor–patient relationship is confidential, Mr Madden.'

'I understand.'

Paul Madden read a folder marked 'Hannah Madden'. His eyes began to fill with tears.

He looked up at Dr Fenton. 'Hannah was pregnant?'

'Yes, when she came to me.

'She wanted to be sure. She was about six weeks into the pregnancy.'

'But there was nothing about pregnancy in the coroner's report.'

'No, Mr Madden, because Hannah wasn't pregnant when she died.

'When she came to me four months ago, she was seeking confirmation. When she came for sleeping pills she was no longer pregnant.

'She'd had an abortion.

'She was very low.'

Paul Madden sat staring at the floor in Dr Fenton's office.

'When you confirmed Hannah was pregnant, how did she take it?'

'She was full of questions. Wanted to know what she could expect over the coming weeks.'

'Did she ask about an abortion?'

'No. I was quite surprised when I found out she'd had one.'

'Did she say who the father was?'

'No.'

'How do I find out who performed the abortion?'

Dr Fenton told him that Hannah's Medicare records might help, but that if it was paid for privately there would only be records with the doctor or hospital that had carried out the procedure.

'Hannah may not have wanted it known, Mr Madden.'

Paul Madden rose, shook Dr Fenton's hand. 'Thank you, Doctor.'

He left the surgery.

The text from Lizzie gave two names. Samuel Jacobson, who was the CEO, and Phillip Novak, who was the chairman of the board.

The company name was Solar4U Pty Ltd.

Paul Madden googled both men.

Samuel Jacobson was prepared to speak to Paul Madden.

His Facebook page hadn't been touched for months, except for an entry headed 'Changing direction' above a photo showing Samuel Jacobson outside an inner-city community centre.

Paul Madden had messaged him and asked for a meeting.

He'd explained his daughter was the person at McGregors who had uncovered the fraud. That his daughter was now dead and he was trying to come to terms with her death.

Samuel Jacobson replied immediately, suggesting a time for the next morning.

They met at the community centre. Samuel Jacobson was filling a box with cans of food and fresh vegetables.

'Hello, Mr Jacobson, I'm Paul Madden. I appreciate you seeing me.'

Samuel Jacobson closed the box and turned to Paul. 'How can I help?'

'Is there anything you can think of that might help me to understand my daughter's death? I know it's a long shot.'

'I'm sorry, but I didn't know your daughter, Mr Madden. I only dealt with the managing director, Terry Marr.

'Once the fraud was revealed, we both wanted the problem sorted quickly and discreetly. The trouble is this kind of thing always gets out.

'It was my fault. I should have been more hands-on.

'But we were doing well, so why worry? Turns out a couple of my more ambitious staff thought helping the company increase profits would win them kudos.'

'You seem very calm about it, Mr Jacobson.'

'You know what this place is, Mr Madden? It's a place that helps those in need. People who are unemployed. Homeless. People whose lives are pretty fucked.'

Samuel Jacobson took another box and began filling it.

'So filling boxes makes me feel good. It has an immediate impact. Someone's life is better for a moment. It's a long way from making decisions that may or may not have an effect on people's lives.

'I have to work hard to make amends.

'My wife and I have separated. Hopefully I can put that back together sometime.

'I can't help you, Mr Madden.

'Sorry.'

Paul Madden and Samuel Jacobson shook hands.

'You can be proud of your girl, Mr Madden. She did what was right. I appreciate that. I really do.'

Then Samuel Jacobson returned his attention to the box he was filling.

Paul Madden sat in his car and thought about Hannah's actions in uncovering the fraud.

And he wondered when an action ended.

If ever.

Phillip Novak was a different kettle of fish.

It was as though he had dropped off the face of the earth.

No LinkedIn profile, no Facebook or Twitter account.

Solar4U wasn't helpful: 'Sorry, we cannot release personal information on our staff.'

'But Mr Novak no longer works for you. It's urgent I contact him.'

'Sorry.'

However, the electoral roll revealed a Phillip Novak lived at Bellevue Hill in Sydney's Eastern Suburbs.

A rather well-off neighbourhood would be an understatement.

The front of the house was walled.

Paul Madden pressed a buzzer.

Nothing happened.

He tried again.

Nothing.

The sound of a lawnmower could be heard coming from the back of the house.

Paul Madden heaved himself over the wall and walked around to a large manicured lawn where a giant of a man was pushing a mower.

'Hello,' Paul Madden said.

The giant stopped and turned to face him. 'Who the fuck are you? And what the fuck are you doing in my yard?'

Paul Madden walked up to the giant. Stopped in front of him. He was a size, that was for sure.

'My daughter worked for McGregors. She died a month back.

'She's the one who discovered the fraud that was taking place with Solar4U and I hoped you might be able to answer a few questions for me.'

'That little bitch. Good fucking riddance. Now fuck off.'

Paul Madden, Vietnam vet, delivered his fist smack into the face of the giant. Right into the bridge of the giant's nose.

Blood squirted and the giant went down onto his back. Paul Madden pressed his foot down onto the neck of the giant, who was now snivelling. 'Don't hurt me. Please don't hurt me!'

'Listen to me carefully.

'I know death.

'I have seen death.

'I am not scared of death.

'But you are.

'So you have a choice.

'You can answer my questions and then I will be on my way. Or you can decide not to answer my questions, in which case I will pummel your spoilt fucking face into the ground.

'What do you reckon?'

The giant whimpered and nodded. 'Okay.'

But it turned out Phillip Novak had bugger-all to tell.

'I'm fucked,' he said. 'Kicked out of the golf club, the yacht club, even the Qantas Chairman's Lounge. Untouchable. All thanks to . . .'

He stopped and looked at Paul Madden.

'Sorry. I didn't mean that.

'It wasn't your daughter's fault.'

Paul Madden looked down at the giant.

'Can I please get up?' the giant asked.

'Not until you tell me everything.'

Phillip Novak swallowed. 'If I tell you, will you go and leave me alone?'

'Try me.'

'I went to your daughter's home.'

Paul Madden raised his foot.

'Please don't! I didn't touch her. In fact I never saw her. I was angry. So fucking angry. And I knew if I saw your daughter I might do something stupid.

'So I left.'

'How did you get my daughter's address?'

'I badgered Terry Marr. He gave it to me.'

'That it?'

'True that's it. Except I'm fucked.'

Paul Madden turned and walked off.

'Mr Madden?'

Paul Madden turned back to face the giant.

'I'm sorry about your daughter.'

'Get to a hospital,' Paul told him. 'Your nose is broken. Tell them you fell off your wall.'

Paul Madden looked through the receipts in the box from Hannah's apartment.

They were well organised, as he would have expected. All tagged.

Petrol receipts, mostly from the Caltex up the road. Paul guessed she was reimbursed for visits to clients.

Receipts from hairdressers. Bit of a leap, but a girl has to look her professional best.

Being reminded of these moments in Hannah's life was hard.

He put down the receipts.

Calmed himself.

Tears came easily. He would never see Hannah again.

Bank statements showed she was a member of a Pilates and yoga studio.

So much he didn't know.

Medicare receipts. Paul saw the two appointments with Dr Fenton.

He went back to the bank statements and looked at outgoings around the time of Dr Fenton's confirmation of Hannah's pregnancy.

Three hundred dollars had been paid to Strathfield Private Hospital a week after she saw Dr Fenton.

There was a further two thousand dollars withdrawn four weeks later.

It was a cash withdrawal.

Strathfield was only ten minutes from Hannah's apartment.

The receptionist looked up as he entered the hospital foyer.

'Hello. I don't know if you can help me. My name is Paul Madden. My daughter Hannah had a procedure carried out here and I wondered if I could speak to your financial controller. My daughter died a few weeks back and I'm not sure if all the required payments were made. I'm trying to tie up the loose ends, you see.'

'I'm so sorry for your loss, Mr Madden,' said the receptionist. 'I'm sure Mrs Sykes can help you.'

Mrs Sykes smiled up at Paul Madden. She was petite and dressed in a woollen suit.

'My receptionist told me about your daughter, Mr Madden. Please accept my condolences. I have looked at our register and I can see that Hannah was here just on four months ago. But everything has been paid in full. There's nothing owing.'

'That is good news. Thank you, Mrs Sykes. Hannah hated being in debt to anyone. I guess that's what comes from being an accountant.' Paul smiled at Mrs Sykes.

Mrs Sykes smiled back.

'It was a little confusing. Her statements showed she paid three hundred to the hospital. I know that couldn't be the total cost for her procedure but there was no other entry. Obviously her fella must have paid the rest. Is that right, Mrs Sykes?'

Mrs Sykes consulted her computer.

'Yes, two thousand dollars was paid on the day.'

Paul said sadly, 'It was a difficult choice for them, but they both felt it wasn't the right time for kids. I respected their decision.'

'It's certainly difficult for some couples. We see it a lot of course.'

'Of course. And he definitely paid everything?'

Mrs Sykes looked back at her computer.

'Oh yes. Mr Freestone took care of it.'

Paul Madden froze.

'I can confirm that there is nothing else owing, Mr Madden.'

Paul Madden thanked Mrs Sykes and left the room.

He didn't hear the receptionist's, 'Goodbye, Mr Madden.'

He walked out of the hospital and leant against the wall of the building.

Paul Madden closed his eyes and took ten deep breaths.

———

It was brutally hot.

Humid.

And then the rains came.

Pissing down. Like being under a waterfall.

It was late afternoon. A platoon was heading out after dark.

They'd had word from the local village that the Vietcong were settled into an area a mile away.

The villagers could be helpful or not helpful. You were never sure. But this information had been corroborated by intelligence.

Paul was in his tent preparing for the operation. Other soldiers were doing the same. The tent flaps were up and Paul could see one of the kids from the village on the camp's perimeter trudging through the rain. Kids were often hanging around, hoping to get a few quid from the soldiers. Or fruit or chocolate bars.

The kid started walking towards the soldiers. He was about a hundred metres away.

It looked like he was carrying something in each hand. Paul couldn't quite make out what. No one else was paying much attention.

And then he realised. The kid had an AK-47 in one hand and what looked like a grenade in the other.

Paul yelled out.

Other soldiers turned to see what Paul was shouting about.

'Put it down! Put it down! For Christ's sake, put it down!' Paul screamed as he raised his rifle.

Other soldiers started screaming at the boy to drop his weapons.

The boy kept walking, raising the hand that was holding the grenade.

Paul Madden's screaming woke him.

He was in a sweat.

He burst out sobbing.

———

He sat in his car opposite the London.

He'd parked here three days in a row from opening until closing.

No Scott.

But today Scott had turned up.

With three mates. Arrived about two.

It was just on five now and they were moving.

Paul Madden followed Scott to his car parked behind the London. The others had headed down Darling Street.

Paul slammed Scott up against the wall of the pub.

Didn't care if he broke his back.

He didn't, but it must have hurt.

'You lied to me, Scott.

'You lied about Hannah.'

He had Scott by the throat.

Scott was having trouble breathing.

Paul released his grip.

'I didn't lie,' said Scott. 'I just didn't tell you everything.'

'Then what is everything? And you tell me now or I will kill you.'

Scott didn't doubt it.

'Can we get in the car?' he said. 'Someone'll call the cops in a minute.'

Paul Madden and Scott Freestone climbed into Scott's car.

'You got Hannah pregnant.'

Scott Freestone searched for air: 'You've got it all wrong. It wasn't me.'

'Don't lie. You paid for her abortion. And then what? Dumped her?'

Scott Freestone leant forward over the steering wheel.

He took a breath.

'Yes, I paid for Hannah's abortion. But it wasn't me who was the father. She had no one else to turn to. She said she couldn't have the baby, but she couldn't afford to pay for the abortion. She was short on money since her overseas holiday.

'I said maybe her company would advance her, but she said she couldn't go to them.

'So I offered to lend her the money and she promised to pay me back, which she did a month later. Hannah was a great girl. I was happy to help.'

'Why should I believe you?'

'It's the truth.'

Paul Madden stared at Scott Freestone.

As a soldier you learnt to know bullshit. You heard it a lot.

He knew Scott was telling the truth.

'Any idea who the father was, Scott?'

'None. But I know he was important to her.

'She had to have the abortion.

'I got the name of a doctor at Strathfield Private Hospital and arranged for Hannah to see him.

'A week later I drove her there and waited, then I took her home.

'She was a mess after it.

'I stayed with her that night.

'Next morning she was a lot better. Said she'd probably take a day or two off work.

'I left her then and spoke to her each day of the following week.

'Then I didn't see her again until she gave me the two grand, and that was it until she rang the week before her death.'

Paul Madden leant across to Scott Freestone and hugged him.

'Thank you, Scott.'

And then Paul Madden got out of the car.

———

'I bought a bottle of riesling. Can I pour you a glass?'

'Not for me.'

'Maybe later then. I'm having one. I'm excited, I guess. Can't blame me.'

'Can't blame you. I blame me.'

'Why? What do you blame yourself for?'

Paul sat in front of the three boxes.

He slowly went through them all again.

Over and over and over again.

But what was the point? Hannah had her secrets, like we all do.

He had learnt a little of her life.

Her struggles.

Standing up for what was right.

Her warmth.

Her privacy.

Her everyday life.

Her friends.

Paul looked at the photograph taken with workmates at a restaurant.

How often had Paul and Hannah enjoyed a restaurant meal together?

Not a lot.

Paul looked at the photograph.

They all had coloured leis around their necks.

You could see ocean in the background.

'Hello, Lizzie. It's Paul Madden. I'm sorry to disturb you.'

'No worries, Paul. How can I help?'

'I'm looking at a photograph of a bunch of you at a restaurant somewhere. You have coloured leis on and I recognise Hannah, you and Terry, but no one else. Can you remember where it was taken?'

'I think I know the one you mean. That would have been at the company retreat on the Gold Coast a couple of years back.'

'Definitely a couple of years back?' Paul asked. 'Not in the last twelve months?'

'No. We haven't all had a dinner like that since.

'Great fun.

'Hannah loved it. Loved that retreat. Well, the bars anyway.

'We all danced on into the night at that restaurant.'

'Thank you, Lizzie. I won't disturb you again.'

And then Paul Madden ended the call.

———

The kid kept coming. His arm was raised.

The rain was pouring down.

All the soldiers were now screaming at the kid to stop.

And he did.

He lowered his arm holding the grenade and dropped the AK-47 from his other hand. It was going to be okay.

But then the kid moved his free hand towards the grenade.

He was about to detonate the grenade.

The soldiers stood in silence.

A tenth of a second seemed like an hour.

And then a shot rang out.

The kid dropped. Blood flowing into the mud and water.

Paul screamed.

All the soldiers looked towards him.

The screaming continued through the nightmare and into Paul's room.

He was sitting up.

He began to shiver.

It was just on 6 pm.

Paul Madden stood in the shadows of the underground car park.

At 8.15 pm the lift doors opened, emptying out two men.

One went straight to his car. The other, who was on his phone, was moving more slowly.

This was the one Paul Madden wanted.

As the man finished his call and opened the car door, Paul grabbed him in a chokehold.

The man tried to struggle free.

'Into the back seat! No noise!'

Terry Marr stopped struggling. He tried to speak, but couldn't.

'We are going to talk,' said Paul Madden. 'You are going to tell me all about you and Hannah.

'And then I will decide what I'm going to do.

'You will have just enough air to talk, but at any moment I can break your neck.

'Remember that.'

Paul Madden released his grip. Slightly.

'There's nothing to tell,' said Terry Marr. 'I hardly knew Hannah. She was a work colleague.'

'That's one lie. I'm giving you three lies. On the fourth, I'll break your neck.

'Want to try again? Two to go.'

The sweat was pouring off Terry Marr. 'Okay, we went out for a drink a few times.'

Terry Marr's voice was like gravel. His voice box was not operating so well.

'I won't call that a lie, but you'd better tell me more.

'Because it was more than the odd drink, wasn't it?' Paul Madden tightened his grip.

'No. Please, no.'

Paul Madden gave Terry Marr some more air.

'You told me you met Hannah after you moved to Sydney a year ago, right?'

'Yes, that's right. We had a few dinners this year. I was impressed with her handling of the solar panel fraud.

'There wasn't a lot in it.

'I had nothing to do with her death. I swear.'

'That's your three lies.

'You met Hannah a year before that, at a company piss-up on the Gold Coast.

'And you had plenty to do with Hannah's death.

'Next lie I break your neck.'

'Oh God. Please. Alright. We had an affair.

'But I didn't kill Hannah.'

Silence.

'I saw her the night she died.'

And then Terry Marr slumped and began to cry.

Paul Madden took his arm from around Terry Marr's throat.

Terry Marr looked up at him.

'Go on,' Paul said.

'We met at that retreat.

'My father-in-law brought me over to see how I felt about running the office in Australia.

'Hannah and I got on well.

'Nothing happened back then, but I was very attracted to her. And she to me, I guess.

'But I had to return to England and I had no idea what my father-in-law's decision would be, whether or not he would give me the job.'

Both Paul Madden and Terry Marr leant back into the seat.

'When did the affair start?'

'After the solar fraud revelation. I couldn't help myself.

'I thought Hannah would tell me to get lost; she knew I was married.

'But she didn't, and we started seeing each other.

'I guess she thought there was a future for us.

'Maybe I let her believe that.

'But there wasn't. That's what I came to tell her the night she died.'

Paul Madden looked at Terry Marr and saw he was beaten. 'Go on.'

'She cooled it a few months before. I figured she was over me, but then she suggested we see each other again. And we did.

'But I knew it had to end.

'If my father-in-law found out, I was history.

'Goodbye, job. Goodbye, family. I had to end it.'

Paul said nothing.

'That's the truth. Honest.'

The two men looked at each other.

'Hannah was pregnant,' said Paul Madden. 'Had an abortion. The baby was yours. That's why she cooled.'

Terry Marr sat up and turned to Paul Madden: 'I didn't know. She never said anything.'

'Did you love Hannah?'

Terry Marr looked out the window and then back at Paul Madden. 'I honestly don't know. I was flattered that a beautiful young woman could find me attractive. I cared for her, that's for sure.'

'What happened on that last night?'

'I rang her and said I wanted to see her. She was very happy that I'd called. Said she would come to me or meet somewhere.

'I told her I would come to her.

'She was so happy to see me. I wasn't sure how to deal with it.

'She brought out a bottle of wine.

'I had none. She had a glass. Then I told her. She begged me not to end it. When I left she was extremely upset. But she was alive. You have to believe me: I had nothing to do with her death.'

'You had everything to do with her death.'

Paul got out of the car and walked away.

'What are you going to do now?' Terry Marr shouted after him.

But Paul didn't reply.

Paul Madden finished the letter and addressed the envelope:

Mr Hamish McGregor AM

McGregors Pty Ltd

Paul Madden sat in the pew and stared at the cross with Jesus nailed to it.

The confessional door opened and a lady walked out.

Paul went in.

'Bless me, Father. I killed a boy.'

There was silence for a moment. Then the priest spoke. 'And how did this happen?'

'Does it matter, Father? It says, *Thou shalt not kill.*'

'It does.'

'It was during a war, but the boy didn't deserve to die.'

'Did you have a choice?'

'I don't know, Father, but I carry guilt. And I need your forgiveness. God's forgiveness.'

Once again there was silence from the priest's side of the confessional.

'Your action cannot be undone. But it need not lead to a lifetime of guilt.

'You will gain forgiveness by forgiving others.

'Be not afraid.'

Paul Madden stood for a moment in front of the cross.

There were candles alight in a holder where people had made offerings.

Paul took a candle.

He lit the candle and placed it in the holder.

He closed his eyes and made the sign of the cross.

Then he turned and walked out of the church.

Across the street there was a postbox.

From his pocket, Paul Madden took the letter addressed to Hamish McGregor.

At the postbox he paused, looking down at the envelope.

This was Hannah's story. It was also Terry Marr's and Scott Freestone's and Lizzie's and Paul's and others who had participated in Hannah's life.

He tore the envelope in half.

Down the street there was a council rubbish bin. Paul Madden walked to it and threw the envelope into the bin.

VIGILANTE

Ahmed did undercover. So did Joe. They'd been cops together for fifteen years.

But that had all ended five years ago, when Ahmed went inside. For dealing.

Ahmed was a good Muslim boy from a good Muslim home. His dad was so proud when Ahmed graduated from the academy. His son the cop. Fighting for justice.

'Allah loves the just.' Justice stood tall in Muslim values.

Ahmed and Joe met at the academy.

Western Suburbs boy meets Eastern Suburbs boy. East meets West. They used to laugh about that.

Afterwards, Ahmed was sent to Surry Hills, inner city.

Joe was sent to Kogarah, south-western Sydney suburb. Home to the Dragons, greatest rugby league side ever— that's what his comrade coppers told him on day one.

But they stayed in touch, Joe and Ahmed. Swapped stories. About the fucked-ups.

———

Five years into being a cop, Joe was asked if he'd like undercover. He jumped at it. Fitted his nature.

Ahmed was pissed off. He wanted undercover too.

And he got it.

He was sent to join Joe on the Gold Coast. Golden strip just over the border into Queensland.

Things were changing in Oz. Middle Eastern changes. New Aussies from Lebanon, Egypt, Jordan.

Like all migrants, they were looking for a new life and new opportunities. And, like the Irish and Vietnamese and Eastern Europeans before them, some looked to crime. Just another occupation.

That influx created a demand for Middle Eastern cops like Ahmed. Undercover cops like Ahmed. Big problem but. Ahmed's religion meant no grog and no drugs.

Ahmed had thought long and hard about that before he said yes. But 'Allah loves the just' kept going around in his brain.

He was a cop bringing justice to the street. He was needed. Crims had to be caught.

But it didn't take long until the next step.

You had to mix with these maggots. Become their friend. Like them. Get them to like you. See you as one of them.

So having a beer in the pub with a dealer was necessary to deal out justice. And blowing a joint in a back room with a dealer was necessary. Had to nail the maggots.

And sharing a line bonded you.

And the high was pretty good.

Maybe deal a bit. That'd look good to the crims.

A bag.

A kilo.

Then he was gone.

No justifying anymore.

Not when you're a dealer junkie.

Not when you're shootin up.

Ahmed went inside for three years.

Boggo Road. Brisbane jail.

Broke his parents' hearts.

But he lied to them. Told them he was still undercover. That he was going inside to nail a big boy.

Truth was, Ahmed was in a bad way. He was a deadset addict by now.

Joe stayed close. He was a mate. He'd seen it coming. Warned Ahmed. But when the serpent has you, you're fucked.

Ahmed found out he could get anything he wanted inside.

But he didn't want anything inside. He was going to get off the stuff.

The boys inside didn't like that. They love a junkie. A junkie'll do anything you say.

Took a few fuckin awful beatings to convince the boys he was off it.

Four fucked ribs. Four concussions. Ten stitches down the side of his face from a blade. A broken arm.

Main maggot called him a piece of shit.

Eventually they left Ahmed alone. And that's what he wanted.

Two and a half years into his time, he was paroled.

The afternoon before his release, Ahmed walked up to the main maggot.

Big fucker.

His gang snickered. Muttered about Ahmed sucking cocks.

Didn't faze Ahmed.

Walked up to the main maggot. Stood in front of him.

The big fucker smiled.

Thought Ahmed was gonna ask a favour for the outside.

As if.

'I am a man of peace,' said Ahmed. The maggots laughed. 'And I am a man who believes in justice. All I'm asking for is an apology, and then I'll forgive you.'

The main maggot leant into Ahmed's face. 'You want to leave this yard alive, cocksucker, you fuck off now.'

Ahmed wasn't stupid. There would be another day.

Joe found Ahmed a room in Pyrmont, an inner-city suburb of Sydney. Only a single room, but it had a basic cooker. There was a toilet and shower in a bathroom that was more like a cupboard.

Got him a job too. Sort of security.

Joe had left the force and taken over a pub lease in Pyrmont. Ahmed worked there as a bit of a dogsbody. He was very grateful to Joe.

Joe had always wanted to be a cop. Ever since that day.

That day when he was twelve and two kids were bullying him in the street.

'Jews killed Jesus!'

'Jews killed Jesus!'

Joe's family was Jewish.

A cop came up to the three of them. Told them to follow him.

Took them to the Jewish Museum in Darlinghurst. Cop took the boys inside and showed them what had happened. Genocide. Hate.

Joe's grandmother had died in Dachau. Nazi concentration camp.

Cop told the boys how under the Nazis the hate tap had been turned on and left on. He told them how after the war the hate tap had been turned off, but there was still the odd little dribble that got out. Said they should turn it off real tight.

The boys shook hands with Joe. Said it was off for good, the hate tap.

Joe blamed himself a bit for Ahmed getting into strife.

When you're undercover it's special. You're living a lie. The only friends you have are other undercovers. With them you have a chance to relax, let your guard down. But you have to look after each other.

A beer. A bong. Joe had been cool. He had always known when to stop. But he could see Ahmed had a problem stopping.

He visited Ahmed inside. Didn't blow his cover. Just a street dealer visiting an addict mate.

When Ahmed got out, Joe knew he had to help. So he gave him work at the pub.

Two years went by pretty fast. Ahmed would front up around six in the evening and leave at midnight.

Last hour was spent cleaning up and chatting with Joe. Just talking bullshit. Good bullshit.

The days were harder.

Exercise helped. Ahmed needed structure. That's what had got him through his time inside. He had taken ownership of his time. Wasn't going to come out institutionalised, even though he was in an institution.

Once the boys left him alone, Ahmed set up a routine. Kept himself neat. Ironed his clothes. Shaved each morning.

Got work in the library. Read. Found out stuff. Learnt about the mind. The power of the mind. How, if you let it, it can fuck you up.

Worked out. Not just weights. Skipping. Stretches.

Same on the outside. Running. From Pyrmont to Bondi, or to La Perouse on the weekend.

Joined the Surry Hills library. Sat and read.

Visited home. Home was awkward. His mother loved to see him and fed him up. But his dad couldn't let go of the fact that Ahmed had been inside.

He guessed it would always be like that. He'd let his old man down. But Ahmed knew how to fuck that off out of his mind.

The pub was pretty well run and Ahmed had it easy.

He wasn't an authorised security guard. Couldn't get a licence, because of his record. Still, if any troubled brewed, he knew how to step in and suggest a cooling-off period outside.

Bought himself an old Toyota to get around in. Nothing pretty, but Toyotas never give up. Didn't drive to the pub. Mainly used it Sundays on his day off.

He liked his walk home at night, sometimes detouring for a major stroll through Newtown and Enmore. Inner city. Knew all the back streets and lanes. Always lights out before two.

———

It had been a big night in the pub. Always was when the Dragons were playing. Specially against Souths. The Bunnies. Joe hated the Bunnies.

He loved the tribal stuff. Kept you alive.

The Dragons won, so the pub was jumping. A round of free beers for everyone, even Bunnies supporters. Joe was a generous fucker.

It was towards one by the time Ahmed tidied up and headed for home.

Winter's night. Ahmed felt good, even though he hadn't drunk anything. Sort of took in everyone else's good vibes.

Worth a decent stroll before bed he reckoned, so took off on one of his favourite beats. Pulled his hoodie over his head.

Shops were all closed. A few blokes yelling from cars: 'Dragons are poofs.' Who gave a fuck.

The servo on the corner was lights out on the pumps, but there was movement in the office. Ahmed stopped in the shadows.

Once a cop always a cop. You notice stuff. Stuff that doesn't seem right. And something didn't seem right.

A robbery was going down.

Lights in the office were dim, but not out. Two blokes and two knives. And the bloke behind the till shovelling notes and coins into a shopping bag, looking shit-scared.

As one bloke reached for the bag, the other smashed the attendant across the head, sending him down behind the counter.

Ahmed walked in the door. The two blokes turned to him, showing him their knives.

'Nice,' he said.

The two blokes didn't have a clue what to do. 'Get out of our fuckin way.'

Ahmed didn't move. 'Put the bag back on the counter, boys. This isn't smart.'

'Fuck you.'

Then the two of them bolted out the door and dived into a car parked at the pumps.

Ahmed stepped behind the counter and poured a bottle of water over the attendant's head. Slapped him awake.

Then he took a pen from the counter, looked at the picture he'd taken on his phone and scribbled a number on a piece of paper.

'Get on your phone and ring triple zero. And give them this numberplate.' He handed the attendant the piece of paper.

Then Ahmed took off for home. Made it into bed on the tick of two.

It was on the news. And in the papers. Story about a servo robbery and a bloke in a hoodie who led police to the robbers. Two young men arrested. Servo attendant needing stitches.

CCTV footage didn't show the face of the hoodie fella. Too dark.

At the pub all the punters were talking about it. Current affairs shows had the footage. Asked if anyone could identify the fella who stood up to the robbers.

Ahmed had a baseball cap on tonight, not his hoodie.

He felt very good. 'Allah loves the just.'

Ahmed had lunch with his mum and dad the next Sunday.

His mum was all over him.

His dad wasn't. Wanted to know when he'd stop working around alcohol. Wanted to know when he'd be more like the man who scared off the robbers in Pyrmont. *That* man's parents would be proud.

His mother told him to be careful with such goings-on around where he lived.

'I'll be careful, Mum. Promise.'

Then Ahmed kissed his mum and left.

————

Trish Bennett didn't like her life.

Hadn't liked it for a long time. Very long time. Been on the streets for a long time.

Started out all right. She got born.

And that was about the end of the good stuff.

Trish's mum was good-lookin. Her dad was a muso on the way up.

Her mum wasn't musical. Couldn't even hum. But her looks got her into the crowd. The on-the-way-up crowd. Very important to be a part of that on-the-way-up crowd.

Then Dad pissed off.

New dads began to come around. On-the-way-up dads. Always leaving her on-the-way-down mum.

Some of the dads started to notice Trish. She was growing up. Fags. Joints. Grog.

One dad hung around. Bit of violence against Mum. Started showing too much interest in Trish. Some pills. Some lines. Some touching.

Mum threw Trish out, not the dad.

Trish found her tribe on the street. Coloured-hair tribe. Piercings tribe. Smoking, swearing, self-harming tribe.

Bit of this for a bit of that. The 'that' wasn't always nice. And that's what was going on now.

In the back of the car. One bloke in the front watching. The other bloke in the back. He had the stuff. If she behaved nicely.

She'd been pretty out of it at some house in Bronte. Bunch of them.

She'd left before midnight. Got a bus to the Cross. Knew a few places she could crash. Could hardly walk when she got out of the bus.

Then this car had pulled up beside her. She'd got in.

But now she wanted to get out. Started yelling.

Got a smack for her trouble. So now she screamed. In his face.

It was surreal. That was the only word for it, Trish reckoned. Or unreal. Whatever. It sure didn't feel real. More terrifying.

Suddenly, the bloke in the front seat was having his head lifted and smashed into the steel rim of the door window. Then it was being lifted again and slammed down. He sagged lifeless.

The bloke in the back seat opened the door. He had one leg out and was rising.

Trish had seen a figure move around the front of the car and now watched as the car door slammed shut onto the leg and into the guts of the bloke getting out.

Then the door was pulled open again and the bloke was grabbed and smashed in the face by a large fist. Three times. He sagged lifeless.

Ahmed reached inside the back seat and helped Trish out.

'Please don't hurt me,' she said.

'I won't hurt you. I'm taking care of you.'

Ahmed reached into the back seat and picked up Trish's bag.

Took out his phone and photographed the numberplate.

Then he led her to an old Toyota.

'Get in the car.'

Trish did as she was told.

The Toyota drove to Pyrmont. Parked around the corner from Ahmed's room. Never park in front of where you're going. Old rule. Old rules die hard.

Ahmed opened the door to his room and gestured for Trish to enter. Once they were inside, he deadlocked the door.

'Sit down,' he said.

'Where?'

'Bed would be most comfortable I'd reckon.'

There was a small sofa, but it was covered in shit. Papers. Food cartons. Clothes.

'Excuse the mess. I can be a bit slack on the weekend.'

Trish sat on the side of the bed. Eyes on Ahmed.

'Tea?' he asked.

'Coffee?'

'I got instant.'

'That'll do.'

Ahmed boiled water. Took a bottle of milk out of the fridge. 'Milk?'

'No thanks.'

Trish watched Ahmed make the coffee.

He handed her a cup. Made room on the sofa. Sat down. They sipped their coffees.

'Big night,' he said.

'Could say that. Could say shitty night. Whatever.'

Trish took another sip of coffee. Looked at Ahmed. 'What happens now?'

'Whatever you like. Stay here until you feel better. I'm happy for you to crash until morning if you want.'

Trish took another sip. 'Where will I crash?'

'On the bed probably a good idea.'

'And you?'

'Here on the couch.'

'Sure you will. You'll want something for getting those fuckwits off my back. I know how it works.'

Ahmed looked at Trish. 'I'll be sleeping here.'

Trish looked at Ahmed. 'This'll be a first.'

Ahmed showed her the toilet and shower. Told her that, if she wanted to leave before he woke, she should shake him and he'd undo the deadlock on the door.

Ahmed waited until Trish had finished in the bathroom before he switched off the light.

'Thanks. I'm Trish.'

'Ahmed.'

It was just before two.

———

Morning.

Trish was still in dreamland when Ahmed put on the kettle. Reckoned he wouldn't want to be in any of her dreams.

Figured she'd need something to eat when she woke. Checked her. Still asleep. Let himself out.

Bought a couple of croissants at the corner cafe and two coffees. Black for Trish. Ahmed was a latte drinker.

When Ahmed returned to the room Trish was dressed and sitting on the edge of the bed.

'Try to get out?' he asked.

'Yep.'

'Deadlocked. Need a key.'

'Why'd you want to keep me here?'

'Thought a feed first might be a good idea.'

Ahmed handed Trish the croissant and coffee.

Ahmed and Trish ate and drank in silence.

'Thanks, I needed that. I'll be off now.'

Trish got to her feet and headed to the door. Stopped. Turned to Ahmed.

'It's not deadlocked now,' he told her.

Trish opened the door. 'Thanks, Ahmed. You one of them Muslims?'

'Maybe.'

'Whatever. Doesn't matter to me.'

Trish turned to leave.

'You get into trouble again, need a bed, you can come here,' Ahmed told her.

Trish walked away.

Ahmed closed the door.

Ahmed thought about Trish. Thought about the lives people lead.

He'd seen a lot of lives. Fucked-up lives.

Glad he'd cleaned up when he did. Nearly a fucked-up life. As they say, 'When you mix with the shit for too long you become the shit.'

Ahmed told Joe about Trish. Gave him the numberplate. Asked Joe to get an address for it.

Joe said he would. Still had mates in the force.

He also said to be careful. Responsibility is a big deal.

Next Sunday, Ahmed drove out west to see his mum.

Parked near the mosque. Watched his old man go in.

Prayer time.

Went every day. Solid.

Recognised a bunch of the fellows going in.

Envied them. They knew who they were.

Ahmed still didn't.

Didn't stop his mum being all over him.

About a month later Ahmed got home after work to find Trish sitting by his door.

She looked crook. Dark eyes. Hair ragged. A mess.

'Hi,' he said.

He opened the door and helped her inside.

She sat on the bed and started shaking. Crying.

'Want to tell me?'

She didn't look at him.

Ahmed got a flannel and, after rinsing it under hot water, passed it to her. 'Wipe your face might help.'

'Ta.'

Trish sat quietly. 'I've fucked up pretty bad. Didn't have anywhere else to go.'

Ahmed sat on the sofa. 'Using?'

'Yep.'

'Wanna stop?'

'Yes. And no.'

Ahmed sat beside Trish. 'I've been there.'

Trish looked into Ahmed's eyes.

'Want me to help?' he asked.

Trish nodded.

———

Vadim and Eric had been driving around looking for Trish for the last couple of nights.

'Where are you, Trishy, you little trollop? We got some lolly for you. You know you like lolly.'

Eric loved the word 'trollop'. His old man used it about his mum when he'd come home from the pub with a skinful. 'You call this dinner, you trollop?'

Then Eric's dad would hurl his dinner plate onto the floor.

Eric reckoned he came from a pretty stable family life. His grandfather was a crim. His old man was a crim. Couldn't get more stable than that.

His old man always said, 'Make sure you find something you like doing.'

He also said, 'There'll always be a price for doing what you like.' He did ten years.

Vadim was named after the famous French film director, Roger Vadim. His mother loved the film *And God Created Woman*. It starred a French beauty called Brigitte Bardot.

Vadim's mum wanted to be Brigitte Bardot. His mum was no beauty, though. Any bloke with an accent had access to Vadim's mum.

Vadim and Eric had covered the city. All the little holes a trollop might venture into. But no Trish.

'Where the fuck is she?'

She was meant to have met them back of the Cross. Deal was she would find some new fuck-ups for them. Fuck-ups like her.

She'd convinced the two of them that she had no idea who it was had smashed them. Said the man had abused her and left her in an alley.

Vadim and Eric had believed her. Why wouldn't they?

But for the past few weeks she'd been vacuuming dope and she was into the boys for a fair bit of dough.

'Payback time. Start dealing and keep your habit.'

She said she was in.

But now the trollop was nowhere to be found.

———

Ahmed told Joe he needed a week off from the pub. Personal stuff.

Joe was cool.

First couple of nights Trish couldn't stop shaking. Like she had no control over her body. In and out of sleep.

Ahmed sat on the sofa watching her. Had a plastic bucket by the bed. Needed emptying a fair bit.

'I fuckin hate you, Ahmed. You fuckin Muslim.' Then she'd start crying. 'You only want me better so you can fuck me.'

Ahmed watched her. Helped her to the loo. Wiped her arse.

'Why you doing this, Ahmed?'

Helped her back to bed.

'Who are you, you fuck?'

And Trish would sit up in bed staring at him.

Ahmed would feed her tissues for her runny nose. Massage her arms and shoulders. Grab some shut-eye when he could find it. When she'd dropped off.

She'd ask him for something to eat but throw up what he gave her.

Green tea helped. Soothed her a little. Calmed the anxiety.

'I gotta get out of here. You've got me locked up. You don't own me. I gotta get out.'

Ahmed talked quietly to her.

Told her about his big sister. How she was almost killed in a car crash. Hooning about with friends when she was fifteen. Ahmed was eleven at the time. The accident had changed them. It reminded them that there was a world out there to enjoy.

Ahmed could help Trish now. Help her to find that world.

On the fifth day he suggested they take a little walk. Was she up to it?

She thought so. She'd slept better that night.

Ahmed put her under the shower. Couldn't get over how small she'd become.

Her clothes had been washed. She thanked him.

They went outside.

The sky was blue. A sunny winter's day.

Trish was wearing one of Ahmed's jackets. She was almost lost in it.

She pulled it tight round her. Smiled at Ahmed.

They sat in the corner cafe and ate. Didn't talk. Just sat.

Ahmed paid the bill. 'Let's walk. Not far. Exercise will do us both good.'

'Sure.'

Trish took Ahmed's arm and they walked.

The next couple of days Trish started to eat more. Kept it down.

Now she slept. Lots.

And they walked more. And longer.

Trish was looking stronger.

On the Sunday Ahmed took the Toyota for a run. Took Trish down the south coast for the day.

Kiama. The blowhole. Ocean comes belting in under the cliff and spouts out through a hole at the top.

On a big day it's something to behold. That day was average.

But Trish loved it. Ahmed had to hold her to keep her from falling down the hole.

She laughed.

Fish and chips from the kiosk. Vacuumed them down.

Ahmed laughed.

Trish watched the seagulls circling for scraps. 'What was your sister's name?'

'Sarah.'

'Did she look like you?'

'Luckily not. She was beautiful.'

'What colour hair?'

Ahmed didn't answer.

'Black, of course. Stupid me. Course it would be black.'

'Yeah, black.'

'I won't ask about her if you'd rather I didn't.'

'No, that's okay.'

'What happened?'

He told Trish how Sarah went into a dark place after the accident. Got in with a bad crowd.

But eventually she saw the light.

Wasn't easy. Had to dig deep. He was proud of her.

She was bright and started studying again. Had a job now that she loved. Primary school teacher.

'I'd like to be a primary school teacher.'

'I'm sure you will be. Bet you'll make a great teacher.'

They took a quiet drive back to Pyrmont.

Trish spent most of the drive looking at Ahmed.

Monday they walked some more and had lunch at Circular Quay, watching the ferries.

'Must be great riding a ferry to work I reckon,' she said.

Ahmed admitted he had never been on one.

'Will we go on one?' she asked.

'Not now. Bit cold. Maybe tomorrow?' Ahmed promised.

Ahmed was meant to work Monday night.

'You want me to get the night off? How you feeling?'

'I'm good. You go. I'm not going anywhere. You can deadlock if you want.'

'Should I?'

'Whatever you like.'

Ahmed made a little spaghetti before he left. Gave Trish a few books to check out.

'Won't be reading much. Too tired. Looking forward to crashing.'

'I'll try to be quiet when I get back.'

'Okay. Night.'

Ahmed closed the door.

He didn't deadlock it.

Ahmed enjoyed working at the pub. Enjoyed the relationship he had with Joe.

They laughed a lot. Silly stuff.

Ahmed was cleaning up before knocking off when Joe handed him an address. He'd had the numberplate traced like Ahmed asked.

'Don't do anything stupid.'

Ahmed smiled at Joe. 'Not me, mate.'

Ahmed wasn't sure what he'd find when he got back to his room.

But Trish was still there, curled up asleep in the bed.

Ahmed stood for a while staring at her. He was glad she hadn't left.

That serpent can hang on for a fair while once it's taken a bite.

Ahmed undressed and settled down on the sofa.

He looked at the address he'd been given. It was in Earlwood. Few ks away. Not far.

Ahmed lay awake, thinking for a bit.

Then he switched off the light.

It was just on two.

When Ahmed woke, Trish was gone.

He checked the bathroom. It was empty.

Maybe she was getting coffee and croissants.

Ahmed knew that was bullshit. Trish had gone. Properly gone.

Ahmed stayed in the flat until it was time for work.

Just in case.

For the next week, Ahmed felt something had left his body.

He couldn't smile.

He couldn't get angry.

He felt no emotion. He was lost.

He did his walk each night through the back streets. Not looking for her.

Yeah, looking for her.

Bit like a zombie.

'What am I—a fucking zombie?'

By Sunday things had changed. He got active.

Took the Toyota to Earlwood. To the address Joe had given him.

The car was in the drive.

Ahmed waited. Nothing happened all day.

About nine o'clock that night the car took off.

Ahmed followed. Around the Cross. Through the inner city. Stopping. Clients picking up. Paying.

Went on until after midnight. Then back to Earlwood.

Lights off.

Ahmed went home.

Next day Ahmed went back to Earlwood.

Early.

Hung around again.

Midday, Vadim and Eric drove down to the Earlwood shops. Parked and went up the stairs to Guys Gym, above a drycleaner's.

Ahmed followed. Baseball cap on.

Not that the two blokes would have seen Ahmed when he bashed the shit out of them.

Told the bloke running the place he'd like to have a look around. Thinking of signing up.

Vadim and Eric weren't working out.

They were in the office with two other blokes.

One of the blokes Ahmed recognised. What were the odds? It was the main maggot from Boggo Road.

Something was going down. Something bad. Had to be if that maggot was involved.

Ahmed left them to it.

What was he after?

Fucked if he knew.

Next two nights Ahmed started driving after work.

Looking for Trish.

Thought he saw her a few times. But out-of-it girls all look the same.

He'd park the car. Walk the haunts.

No chance of lights out by two. Lucky to be home by sun-up.

Ahmed couldn't shake it. He needed to know.

So, back to Earlwood.

It was Sunday. Day off.

Like hell.

Stakeout.

Vadim and Eric drove off mid-afternoon. With purpose.

Up through the Cross. Along New South Head Road. Through Double Bay. Point Piper. Rose Bay. Ex-prime minister's patch.

Finally Vaucluse.

Money. Money. Money. You could smell it.

Then they were onto Old South Head Road and took a side street.

Stopped. Walked up to a gated house. Two storeys. High fence all around it. No seeing in.

Vadim and Eric pressed an intercom.

Then the gate opened and they walked in.

Ahmed had parked a bit along. He sat and watched. For an hour. Maybe more.

Eventually the gate opened.

Vadim and Eric walked back through the gate to the car with two gorillas, each gorilla carrying a suitcase. Suitcases went into the boot.

The gorillas shook hands with Vadim and Eric. Watched as they drove off.

The gorillas were back inside when Ahmed set out to follow.

———

Trish knew she was fucked.

Tried to kid herself, while she was with Ahmed, that she could shake that fucking serpent. But she knew she couldn't.

It had been early when she'd lit out from Ahmed's.

She was busting. Needed something now. Now, now, now.

So she got it. Friend from the Cross.

Felt great.

Her friend said she could crash there for a week. The friend was going to Brisbane to see her mum to get money for dope. Said Vadim and Eric would be around. They would see her right.

Trish knew she was fucked. She knew she was never going to be a primary school teacher.

———

Ahmed polished off a steak at a restaurant opposite Guys Gym. That's where Vadim and Eric had driven to with the suitcases.

Took one suitcase into the gym. Brazen.

It was after nine when they left Guys to drive home.

Ahmed followed. Stayed watching for an hour, then pissed off.

Walked the streets some more.

Why?

In bed by two.

Couple nights later at the pub on the nightly news on TV the cops were asking for help identifying a young girl found dead of an overdose up at the Cross.

Showed a photo.

It was Trish.

Ahmed felt the rush through his body.

Felt he'd let Trish down.

Felt angry. Very.

Ahmed didn't make it to bed by two. He was up all night. Had things to do.

Really fuckin important things to do.

The Toyota was a busy little car.

Fair bit of driving and stopping.

Stop one: Guys Gym.

They had parking around the back and stairs leading up to the gym.

Ahmed opened the door. It was just on 11 pm.

The gym was empty, but the office light was on.

The maggot looked up from behind the desk as Ahmed walked in. 'Gym's closed, mate. Opens at ten tomorrow.'

Ahmed sat opposite the maggot. 'Remember me?'

And the maggot did. Went straight to the drawer in the desk.

Ahmed slammed the drawer shut on the maggot's hand. He screamed.

Then Ahmed smacked him across the face with a dumbbell.

The maggot fell out of his chair onto the floor. Be a while before he woke up. How cool is karma?

Ahmed shoved cardboard and papers into the middle of the room, along with mats and whatever else would burn.

Then he set them alight.

Picked up the office phone and rang 000: 'Fire in Guys Gym, Earlwood. Better hurry—could get out of hand.'

Stop two: Vadim and Eric's place.

It was after midnight and the lights were out, but the car was in the drive.

Ahmed smashed the side window of the car and poured petrol inside. Lit a match.

Walked to the front door and bashed on it.

'Hey, mate, your car's on fire. Better get out here.'

As they scrambled out the door the dumbbell collided with their noses. Down they went.

Ahmed dragged them inside and tied them to a bed each.

Reckoned the neighbours would be calling the cops pretty soon.

Stop three.

Ahmed had googled petrol bombs before he'd set out.

Pretty easy. A bottle. Petrol. A wick. And a light.

He'd made four of them.

They sailed over the gate of the Vaucluse mansion, crashing through windows.

Started a blaze.

Hell of a blaze.

Bloody big blaze.

Next night at the pub it was all over the news.

Was on the morning radio, too.

In the papers.

Three incidents.

Had to be drug related.

Fire at an Earlwood gym.

Firefighters found illegal substances and weapons while attending to the fire. Charges were laid against the owner. Showed him being shoved into a police car. The main maggot.

A second fire in Earlwood after a car exploded in the driveway of a home.

A quantity of drugs were found by police. The front lawn of the house was covered in snow. Inside two men were found tied to their beds. Gags in their mouths. Both had broken noses.

A third incident in the exclusive Sydney suburb of Vaucluse. A mansion was engulfed in flames during the night.

Once again firefighters and police found a large supply of drugs, plus more than four million dollars in cash. Was thought to be a major breakthrough in exposing a criminal gang of drug importers. Charges were being laid.

Joe and Ahmed were standing by the door of the pub watching the telly. The Dragons game had been stopped for an injury.

Joe turned to Ahmed. 'Someone was busy.'

'Looks that way.'

'That car numberplate was registered in Earlwood, wasn't it?'

'Was it? Dunno. Lost the piece of paper.'

Joe smiled. 'Be careful, mate.' Then he moved off.

Game was back on. Dragons won.

'Round on the house.'

The punters swarmed the bar.

Joe winked at Ahmed.

Ahmed nodded.

Ahmed sat up front of the Manly ferry.

It was a beautiful Sydney morning. Shimmering harbour. Winter light.

Thought about Trish. How it was meant to be.

Thought about how good he was at making up stuff about his life. You'd better be if you were undercover.

Would have liked to have had a sister. Being an only child was sort of lonely.

He knew it was time to leave the pub. Time to get back to who he was.

Ahmed.

Not some false life.

'Allah loves the just.'

Might go to the mosque with his dad.

His dad would like that.

SWEET JIMMY

Janine was bowling with friends at the Hurstville ten pin bowling alley when she came across Jimmy.

He was with his brother. They could have been twins. Jimmy was a year younger than Johnny.

The boys were in the lane next to Janine and her friends.

Got talking.

Got competitive.

Jimmy and Johnny were good.

Janine wasn't so good, so Jimmy said he'd show her if she'd like.

She said sure.

Jimmy came into Janine's lane. Got behind her.

Put one hand around Janine's waist and held her wrist with the other.

Janine felt an excitement she'd never felt before.

Jimmy swung her arm back gently and then forward, moving with her.

Janine let go of the ball.

She knocked six pins down. Best ever.

At the end of the game Jimmy and Johnny invited the girls to burgers and chips at the cafe across the road. They said they had plenty of money. It was their shout.

How could the girls say no?

Really hard to say no to Jimmy.

Janine was sixteen when she met Jimmy Quigley. Jimmy was seventeen.

Just.

He had the gift of the gab.

He made her laugh.

There wasn't a lot of laughing in her house. It wasn't all bad. But a lot of yelling with her mum and dad.

Always yelling.

It seemed like that anyway. That made it hard for Janine to study. And Janine was a hard worker. She wanted to do well. Not like some of the other girls, who were only interested in boys.

Janine liked boys, but not all the time.

This was her last year of school and she had plans. Nursing.

Couple of extra years of study after high school and then she'd be straight into it.

Janine admired nurses. She loved how they looked after people.

Liked that they wore uniforms too. Crisp and clean.

Nothing much crisp and clean at home. Not a pigsty, but messy.

Hard for Mum with three kids.

And Dad was useless. Made everything messier.

Never picked up.

Never put anything away.

Never turned off lights.

He loved Janine though. So did her mum.

It was just that everything was messy.

Janine was off mess.

Nurses weren't messy.

Jimmy started calling on Janine. He got on great with her mum and dad.

Mum said he was a real gentleman. Please and thank you goes a long way.

But Mum would only let Janine out during the day on weekends, and only after all her homework was finished.

Jimmy didn't have a car so they would get the train to places. Sometimes even a taxi.

Jimmy loved spending money on Janine. Bought her perfumes and stuff, and always flowers for her mother.

Then Jimmy got a van, with *Jimmy the Electrician* written on the sides. Janine was so proud of him.

Even though they could only go out during the day didn't mean they couldn't kiss and cuddle and stuff.

Not a lot of 'stuff' stuff. Janine wouldn't let Jimmy go too far. Called him her 'sweet Jimmy'. It was exciting, though. She told her girlfriends. They were jealous.

Now Jimmy had a van with a mattress in the back.

Mum and Dad didn't know about the mattress.

It was getting harder to say no.

Jimmy Quigley told Janine that he loved her, and Janine told Jimmy that she loved him.

She had never felt this good. Like she wanted to burst.

Like she couldn't concentrate. Couldn't think.

Couldn't think about anything except Jimmy Quigley.

That had to be love, she reckoned.

She knew Jimmy really wanted it.

He told her. But only when she was ready.

The day would come, she knew that.

Some of the girls at school had done it.

It scared her.

It so excited her.

And then one Sunday they went to Garie Beach for a picnic. In the Royal National Park, about an hour south. Beautiful place.

Janine made up a picnic lunch.

Smoked salmon sandwiches with tomato and pepper. And apple juice. Jimmy loved smoked salmon.

And peaches and strawberries.

They swam in the ocean.

So blue.

Mucked about. Splashing each other.

Jimmy put Janine on his shoulders and then they fell into the surf.

They kissed in the surf.

Jimmy's body felt so good.

Strong.

No one else on the beach. All to themselves.

And it happened.

Jimmy didn't force it.

It just happened.

Had to happen.

Janine cried after it and then kissed Jimmy all over his face.

Wasn't love wonderful?

Her sweet Jimmy.

Jimmy said he'd be careful. And he was. But each time it was harder to be careful.

The mattress got a bit of a workout.

Couldn't keep their hands off each other.

'Love you.'

'I love you more.'

'No, I love you more.'

And then they would laugh and kiss.

So happy. So excited.

It was a Saturday, and Janine and Jimmy were shopping at Bondi Junction.

Janine started to cry.

Jimmy hugged her to him. 'What's up?'

Janine didn't say anything. Just kept hugging Jimmy.

'What's up?'

And she told him.

Told him she was pregnant. Told him she was sure. Told him she hadn't had her period for eight weeks now.

'What will you do?'

'Tell Mum, I guess. Have to.'

And they did, together.

Janine kept going to school until she was showing.

First few months were difficult. Morning sickness they called it. Had trouble keeping anything down.

At five months school was over.

Janine's mum and dad weren't keen on Jimmy visiting, but Janine wanted to see him.

It was awkward. They would go for walks and talk about the future.

Jimmy said that he would marry Janine.

That he would be a good father.

He said he'd talk to Janine's dad about it.

Then he got a call to come to the house for a meeting with the social worker. What the fuck did his and Janine's baby have to do with a social worker?

They sat in the lounge room. Janine, her mum and dad, Jimmy and this woman, the social worker.

And they told him.

Janine would have the baby and then it would be adopted out.

Immediately.

Jimmy told them he wanted to marry Janine.

Janine's dad said he was too young.

Janine was too young. She had her whole life in front of her.

The social worker told them there were families out there longing to adopt babies. Good families that would give the baby a good future. That Jimmy couldn't offer that. He was too young. It would be stupid to think he could.

'Stupid? You think I'm stupid?! Who the fuck do you think you are?'

Janine's dad told Jimmy to get out. Not to come and see Janine again.

Jimmy went out to his van. He sat in it. He cried. For himself. Janine. His baby.

Then he drove off.

He never saw Janine again. He couldn't handle the pain. He knew that.

He also knew he'd never forget that fucking social worker. She'd pay.

Somehow.

———

Johnny and Jimmy were working at The Nick when the letter came. It was addressed to Mr Jimmy Quigley, care of The Nick, Tuggerah.

Jimmy opened it.

It was from a brother of Janine. Jimmy stood frozen.

Then blood surged through his body. He started to shake.

Jimmy closed his eyes, tried to settle his emotions.

Then he went to his car. Sat inside and began to read:

Hi Jimmy,

I got your address from your family.

Janine died last week and I knew you'd want to know.

I wasn't sure if you'd been in touch over the years, but while we were cleaning up her things, we found a letter for you.

I enclose it.

Janine's life hadn't been too good for a number of years. Or always really—not since the baby thing, I guess.

I was pretty young back then and didn't know a lot about what happened. Anyway, I know it was pretty heavy and affected Janine in a big way.

Janine took her own life, Jimmy.

Mum and Dad are pretty devastated. It's horrible.

Say a pray for her, will you?

Regards,

Terry

Jimmy could feel the tears flowing down his face. Couldn't stop them.

He sat and waited until there were no more tears, and then he opened the letter from Janine.

My sweet Jimmy.

How are you?

Well and happy, I hope.

There have been so many times when I've tried to write to you but then I'd get too sad and have to stop and throw the letter away.

My life hasn't been so great.

You know I always wanted to be a nurse—well, that didn't happen, not after the adoption. I didn't even finish school.

I'm starting to cry again but I'm going to keep on writing because I may not get another chance.

We had a little girl, Jimmy. She was beautiful. She looked like you Jimmy. Lucky, eh?

They let me keep her for four days. I fed her Jimmy. She'd look up at me. I know she knew I was her mum and that I would look after her.

But I didn't, did I Jimmy? I let them take her away.

They gave me a paper to sign. Mum had to sign it too.

There was a nurse and the social worker, and they just said, 'It's all good now. We've fixed things, you won't have to worry. The little one's gone to a good home.'

And that was it. Mum and Dad took me home and I think I cried for a month.

Jimmy, I have lived a life of pain. Our little girl is out there somewhere. I pray every day that she is alright and being looked after properly. All I can do is hope, but that doesn't stop the pain. We lost our beautiful little girl. It's wrong what they did. That nurse and social worker had no right to take my baby away.

Every time I see mothers laughing and playing with their angels it's like a stab to my heart.

I'm sorry to burden you with these thoughts, Jimmy, but you are our little girl's father and you should know how wrong this was. We could have had a good life together Jimmy, but they wouldn't let us.

I'm not sure what I'll do but I can't handle the pain anymore.

Please think of me and our little girl.

Your Janine xx

Jimmy couldn't move. He sat still in his van. And then he felt the anger rise up in him.

He left the van and walked back to The Nick.

Johnny was laughing with some customers. Jimmy stared hard at them. They all looked the same. They all looked like that cunt of a social worker.

———

'Hello?'

'Hello. Mrs Tierney?'

'Yes, this is Anne Tierney.'

'Hi, Mrs Tierney. I'm ringing from The Nick. You know, the garden centre in Tuggerah.'

'Oh yes, hello.'

'Mrs Tierney, one of our young fellas will be down your way today and we wondered if it would be convenient to pop in and show you some new plants we have in, especially our new orchids.'

'That would be fine. I'm here all day on my own. That would be lovely thank you.'

'He'll see you soon then.'

'Wonderful. Bye.'

The van drew up a street away from Anne Tierney's.

He knocked on the door.

Detective Terry Reynolds was sitting at his desk when the phone rang.

He picked it up.

Listened.

Put down the receiver.

Closed his eyes.

Detective Terry Reynolds stared at the wall.

He'd just had a phone call informing him of Mary Harris's death.

He counted to ten.

Then twenty.

Then one hundred.

Counting always helped.

Got the emotions back in check.

Terry took a drive to Strathfield. Talked to the local cops.

They did a doorknock of houses in the vicinity.

That meant a lot of houses.

They were thorough.

Nothing.

No one had seen anything, bugger-all.

The Strathfield cops had done a good job earlier. They'd photographed the body from every which way. They'd dusted for fingerprints and found none that shouldn't have been there.

The daughter had been the one to discover her mother dead on the lounge. Been dead for a couple of days while the daughter had been finishing a sail through the Pacific.

Two empty tea-cups on the table and a photo album open.

No prints on them. Clean as a whistle. Very careful, this fucker.

Terry spent a day at the house. The clue was there, if there was a clue.

And, of course, there was a clue.

One thing Detective Terry Reynolds was sure of.

Phil Quigley hadn't killed Mary Harris.

Detective Terry Reynolds sat in the waiting room at Long Bay jail.

Phil Quigley was brought in. Prison guard either side and cuffed.

Phil sat on the chair opposite Terry.

'You hear about the killing of the lady in Strathfield?'

Phil nodded. 'Cons want to know how I did it.'

'Funny bastard, aren't you? Well, we know you didn't.'

'Didn't I? Whew, had me worried. That's a relief.'

They sat staring at each other.

'Got a picture of the orchid?' Phil asked.

Detective Terry Reynolds reached into his jacket. Brought out a photo and laid it in front of Phil.

'Classy,' said Phil. 'Moth orchid.'

'Why a moth orchid?'

'Don't ask me. I didn't kill her, you said.'

'Any ideas?'

Phil looked at the photograph in front of him. Smiled. 'People don't like moths much. Try to kill the buggers.'

'Maybe symbolic.'

'Maybe.'

'Know where it might have come from?'

'Can't tell. Could be anywhere. It's been re-potted.'

Detective Terry Reynolds told Phil he had a problem.

He reckoned the person who killed Mary Harris was the same person killed Agnes Heslop and Anne Tierney.

But the person who killed Anne and Agnes was locked up, sitting in front of him, and couldn't have killed Mary Harris.

'That is a problem. So what's your solution?'

'You didn't kill Anne and Agnes.'

'So why am I locked up?'

'Because you pleaded guilty.' Detective Terry Reynolds stared hard at Phil Quigley.

'Why did you plead guilty?'

Phil smiled. 'Cos you said I killed them.'

Detective Terry Reynolds stared hard at Phil Quigley: 'If you didn't kill them, who did?'

Detective Terry Reynolds watched as Phil Quigley was taken back to his cell.

There had to be a serial killer out there.

Detective Terry Reynolds sat in an armchair opposite Daisy Harris and her husband.

Sydney Harbour sat behind him.

That's the thing about being a cop: you get to sit everywhere.

Meth labs, back rooms of strip clubs and even media moguls' mansions, overlooking the greatest harbour in the world.

It was a month since Mary Harris had been murdered. The couple had been questioned a couple of times before.

'I'm not sure how we can help, Detective,' said Daisy. 'We've told you and the officers everything we know. But of course, we'll do anything to help find Mum's murderer.'

Terry Reynolds asked again if there was anyone Daisy could think of who would have wanted to see her mother dead.

Daisy assured him that her mother had no enemies and was well loved.

'It seems your mother was sharing the photos of your wedding over a cup of tea with whoever did it. I know how strange that seems.'

Daisy and her husband agreed that it made no sense.

Terry addressed the husband. 'And you, sir—do you have any thoughts? Perhaps someone who wanted to get back at you?'

The media mogul considered this.

'I have a lot of business enemies, for sure, but none that would want to murder my mother-in-law. That would be bizarre.'

Terry thanked them for their time and started for the door.

'Detective,' said Daisy, 'the papers mentioned that the murder resembled two earlier murders. They called the killer the Orchid Man or something like that. What was his name?'

Detective Terry Reynolds told her his name was Phil Quigley.

'Yes. When I saw that name, because it is a strange name, I remembered years ago going out with a boy for a very little while with a name like that. Johnny Quigley. But that was over ten years ago. I was seventeen. Johnny was maybe twenty.'

Detective Terry Reynolds's brain went: *Bingo*. At last, a door opening.

Detective Terry Reynolds drew up outside Johnny Quigley's unit in Avoca.

He could smell the ocean. Lucky bastard.

Don't get that smell if you're from the suburbs.

Out front were two vans.

Jimmy the Electrician and *Johnny the Plumber*.

It was Johnny the Plumber Detective Terry Reynolds wanted to talk to.

He knocked at the door of the unit. It was opened by Johnny. Terry introduced himself. Said he had a few questions about the death of Mary Harris.

Johnny was pretty sure he'd be of no help, but he took Terry out the back, where Jimmy was swigging a beer. A barbecue was alight.

Terry asked Johnny if he knew Mary Harris.

'Long time ago, mate. Went out with her daughter.'

'Daisy Harris?'

'Yep.'

'How'd you get on with her?'

'Pretty good with Daisy. She was crazy about me. Not so good with the old lady. She barred me from seeing Daisy.'

'Not your favourite person?'

'Like I said, it was a long time ago.'

Detective Terry Reynolds asked about Johnny's whereabouts on the day Mary Harris was killed.

Johnny said he was clearing up at The Nick, given it was closing down what with Phil being inside.

The detective asked Jimmy if he knew Mary Harris.

'No, sir, never met her. Only met Daisy once with Johnny.'

Detective Terry Reynolds asked Johnny if he could come up with a witness to confirm he was where he said he was.

Johnny said the lady who did the accounts at The Nick would vouch for him.

Terry told Johnny not to leave town. Then he went outside and photographed Johnny's van.

———

The doorknock started the next morning. Almost five hundred houses around Strathfield.

'We're investigating the murder of Mary Harris, who lived near here. Can you take a look at this photo, tell me if you remember seeing this van?'

And the cops would present a copy of the photo of Johnny the Plumber's van with a number for Strathfield police.

They also had a photo of Johnny.

'Please keep this, and if anyone from your family remembers seeing the van or this man then contact us on the number shown. Thank you.'

Two days of doorknocking and nothing.

The accounts lady from The Nick rang with an alibi for Johnny. He'd been at The Nick all that day.

The door was closing again.

And then the call.

'My name's Margaret Nolan. I think you should come round and talk to my son.'

———

Margaret Nolan lived in a two-storey house four streets back from Mary Harris's home.

Detective Terry Reynolds knocked on the door. Margaret Nolan opened it and Terry showed his badge.

'Please come in, Detective. My son is upstairs.'

Margaret Nolan led Terry up the stairs to her son's bedroom.

Her son sat at a desk by the window. A computer was open and books were stacked tidily on the desk.

'James, this is Detective Reynolds. Will you tell him what you told me?'

'Sure. That wasn't the right writing, Detective.'

'What do you mean, James?'

'The van in the photo. It had the wrong writing on it. It said *Jimmy*, not *Johnny*.'

'Are you sure, James?'

'You bet. I looked at it because it was parked opposite and I could see it clearly from my desk. And my name is

James, and everyone calls me Jimmy, and I hate that and I wondered if that electrician hated it too. But I guessed he didn't, because he had it plastered all over his van.'

'He had *Jimmy the Electrician* written on the side of his van?'

Detective Terry Reynolds told James Nolan he was a genius. Thanked him and his mother.

———

Jimmy Quigley sat in the plane at Sydney International Airport.

The Qantas flight would be taking off for Bali at any moment.

The doors had been closed and they were waiting their turn on the runway.

Jimmy knew it was time to get out. Bali would do.

He and Johnny had made a couple of trips there over the years.

From there he could get lost in South-East Asia. No one would find him.

It amazed him how Johnny didn't really care about that fucking woman. She'd slammed the door on him.

Another woman taking over, making decisions about other people's lives.

Well, Jimmy had showed Mary Harris what for. And the others—Anne and Agnes.

Playing nice with cups of tea. He knew what they really thought of him.

And there would be more of them overseas. And Jimmy would fuckin show them, like he'd showed those three.

The plane was moving. Be up, up and away soon.

Jimmy looked out the window.

Didn't seem right. They weren't heading for the runway. They were going back to the gate.

Engines shutting down.

Then the door opened and two police officers boarded the plane and walked down the aisle towards Jimmy Quigley.

———

Jimmy Quigley pleaded guilty. Said it wouldn't be safe to let him out.

His sentence was life. Non-parole.

Phil Quigley was charged with hindering a murder investigation but was released due to the time already spent inside.

He reopened The Nick and its popularity increased.

Johnny Quigley stuck to plumbing.

Detective Terry Reynolds was moved further up the chain of command.

There was talk he would one day be Commissioner of Police.

Detective Terry Reynolds thanked God there were kids like James Nolan around.

Read on for a preview of Bryan Brown's new book

Available in November 2023

1

David ditched his bike by the side of the track behind a gummy. Same place as before. Then pulled a bit of bullshit grass and stuff over it.

Better to hide it. Never knew who might be along and David wasn't keen on getting in the bad books with you know who. The drug heavies.

David found the entrance a month or so back when he was pissing about with nothing to do. He'd skipped school cause there was bugger all going on. Always bugger all going on. David didn't blame the teachers. There was always a bloody great racket going on in the classroom. Most of the kids wanted to learn but there was a mob who didn't give a shit and fucked it for everyone else. So the teachers just told you what pages to read and left it at that. So why bother going?

Moira would whip him if she knew.

She wasn't gonna know. He'd be back before dark.

Thing he did love learning was his language. Indigenous language. And he wanted to improve. You bet he did. And he was getting good at it. Gumbaynggir was his mob. Funny how if there's something you want to learn then the easier learning is. David tried to explain this to his older brother Wayne but Wayne wasn't ready. He didn't have time to learn. Bit of a silly bugger was Wayne. Kept getting into strife. But he was starting to quieten down now. Had to, Moira said.

David thought if he got good enough with his language then one day he could be a teacher. Teach the other kids their language. David loved that idea.

And now David was back here deep in the forest.

Because last time he found the shed.

And he wanted another look.

You had to be bloody careful being out this far. So many padlocked gates. DO NOT ENTER. And guns for sure.

But David was smarter than the average fuckwit. He knew how to be sneaky. It was in his blood. Silent as.

Last time David thought he might find a patch. Gunja patch. Plenty of gunja patches out here in the Parks. National Parks. Get a couple of pockets full. Make a buck.

But.

Better.

He found the shed.

No one about. Just a shack and a shed covered in gal iron.

All closed up.

So sneaky David snuck up for a look. Pretty hard to get a look inside but then he found a hole in the gal.

Wow and didn't he love what he saw. Classic. And now he was back for another look.

And take a picture.

Blow his mates' minds.

David lay on his back and wiggled his way under the barbed wire. Too easy for a blackfella. Then he made his way from gummy to gummy, bent low and quiet. Didn't know who owned the joint but they wouldn't want him there, that's for sure.

There were gummies and bushes almost all the way to the shed. There'd been bloody great bushfires all through the forest but somehow some places escaped the fire. No rhyme or reason. Just however God wanted it. That's if you believed in a god. If not, it was luck. Good or bad. David couldn't believe how fast the forest was coming back. Green shoots everywhere. If you looked closely you could see the black trunks behind the green. Nature was amazing, David reckoned.

He was about to dash to the hole in the gal for a geek when he noticed the van. That wasn't there before. Better be careful. So he was. Stopped. Lay down in the grass and watched.

Lay there. Waited. Nothing going on. And then the door to the shack opened and a big bloke came out, walked around to the side of the shack, bent down and lifted a trapdoor. Heavy steel. Went down steps. Must be a room below.

David thought this was a good time to piss off but he couldn't help himself.

Who was this fella?

Sort of recognised him. Sort of. Could be one of them surfer fellas at the coffee shop. What was that place called? The Basin yeah. A hangout for the old blokes. All looked the same too. Old blokes. Anyway, thought he'd seen him about a couple of times.

And then up came the fella holding a rope. He was leading something. A girl. The end of the rope was tied around her throat. She just followed him. Wasn't fighting or anything. Maybe it was some game. Some adults' game. David had seen porn. Everyone had. Some strange sick stuff goes on there. The fella led the girl to a spot by the shack and tied the rope to an iron stake belted into the ground. The girl sat on the ground while the fella sat a frypan on a steel plate that he swivelled into place. He lit a fire underneath the plate. Then he emptied the contents of a bag into the frypan. And stirred.

The girl said nothing. She was dressed but her clothes looked pretty wrecked. Hanging off her.

Her hair was matted. David couldn't see her face. Then the bloke went inside the shack leaving the girl sitting there. She didn't move. Didn't even look around. Just sat.

David ran to the side of the shed. Keeping down. He had to take a closer look. This was weird, man. Really weird.

David thought maybe the bloke had gone to get plates or something but how long does that take. He was sure taking his time. David watched the girl. No movement. Didn't even move her arms. Still, like a dummy.

David took out his phone and looked through the hole in the gal. Yep, still there. Still a classic. So he snatched a photo then turned the phone off. Didn't want that going off and giving him away.

Where was the bloke? He'd been inside for at least ten minutes. David worried the food would be burnt through. You can't leave stuff burning over a flame without watching it. Moira had told him that.

Where was the bloke?

And then a bag came down over David's head. A rope around his body. Pulled tight.

He couldn't move. Shit scared. Literally.

He felt his bowels open and the shit ran down his leg. David screamed.

He was dragged along the ground. Then picked up.

And now his head was in the water. With a hand pushing it down. Down.

He couldn't fight back. The bloke was too strong. David wanted to grow up strong.

People respected you if you were strong. But he wasn't going to grow up strong. Not now. And he could say goodbye to any more learning of his language.

David knew he was going to die here in this water.

———

When the boy stopped struggling, the bloke pulled him out of the dam. Laid him on the ground. Made sure he was dead. Then he carried the boy past the girl around to the shack. Leant him against the wall.

The girl waited.

Terrified.

And then she heard it.

An almighty wailing.

Loud. From deep down. From the darkest place.

The shack door opened and closed.

When the bloke returned he carried two cups and a plastic container holding water.

He passed one cup to the girl. She took it. She had to look at him. Couldn't help herself. And she had to speak.

'Did you kill the boy?'

'He was an intruder.'

They sat in silence.

He spooned food from the frypan into a bowl and put it by the girl. He poured water into her cup.

She took some water.

'You want more water?'

She nodded her head.

'Didn't hear you.'

'Yes.'

'And?'

'Please.'

He poured water into her cup.

Now she didn't dare look at him. Didn't know if he might lash out.

So she looked at the ground. Kept quiet. Gulped down the food from the bowl. Knew she had to keep it down. Wasn't easy. Never knew how long to the next meal. Sometimes twice a day but not always. Whenever he felt like it.

She wondered what he was thinking. What he was going to do.

It was the first time someone had been to the place. Well as far as she knew.

There may have been others. Sometimes she thought she heard a car but down in the room you could hardly hear a thing.

And if the boy had discovered the place then maybe others knew about it and maybe others would come. And others would find her. And finally she would get out of this hell. She had to hold onto that. The hope that someone would come. She had to hold tight onto that no matter what. It had to end.

The frypan was empty. He poured water onto it, kicked the steel plate to the side and held the pan over the fire. Scraped it with a fork. Cleaned it. Sort of. Then he stood.

'Pour some water on your face. Don't want a dirty face under me, do I?'

Then he went back into the shack with the frypan and bowls.

She wanted to scream.

Scream the forest down.

Scream the whole fucking world down.

But she couldn't.

It would cost too much.

And then he returned.

Took the rope off the iron stake.

'Up.'

She rose.

He led her to the trapdoor.

'Down you go.'

He followed her down.

Then he pulled the trapdoor shut.